C000177120

The Human Kind

The
HUMAN KIND

Alexander Baron

Black Spring Press

Published in 2011 by Black Spring Press Ltd
Curtain House
134–146 Curtain Road
London
EC2A 3AR

www.blackspringpress.co.uk

First published in Great Britain by Jonathan Cape Ltd 1953

Copyright © 1953 Alexander Baron
Introduction copyright © 2011 Sean Longden

The right of Alexander Baron to be identified as the author of this work has been
asserted by him in accordance with the Copyright, Designs and Patents Act 1988.

All rights reserved. Except for brief quotations in a review, this book, or any part
thereof, may not be reproduced, stored in or introduced into a retrieval system, or
transmitted, in any form or by any means, electronic, mechanical, photocopying,
recording or otherwise, without the prior written permission of the publisher.

ISBN: 978-0-948238-47-5

A full CIP record for this book is available from the British Library

Cover design Ken Leeder

Typeset in Calisto by Dexter Haven Associates Ltd, London
Printed and bound in Great Britain by CPI Cox & Wyman, Reading

Also by Alexander Baron

From the City, from the Plough (1948)

There's No Home (1950)

Rosie Hogarth (1951)

With Hope, Farewell (1952)

The Golden Princess (1954)

Queen of the East (1956)

Seeing Life (1958)

The Lowlife (1963)

Strip Jack Naked (1966)

King Dido (1969)

The In-Between Time (1971)

Gentle Folk (1976)

Franco Is Dying (1977)

CONTENTS

Introduction

SEAN LONGDEN

Reading this book brings back many memories for me. Farewell comrade
Corporal Joe Bernstein!

Harry Ratner, Baron's wartime comrade,
upon first discovering his novels, 2011

As an historian, one somehow knows when a novel 'feels right'. Yet, while
the literary bookshelf of World War II is crammed with wartime works
acclaimed as classics, there is just one writer whose work holds its own
against that of the foremost writers of his era but who has given us an
honest and accurate picture of the wartime British soldier. That writer is
Alexander Baron.

As Joseph Alexander Bernstein, he was born on 4 December 1917 in
Berkshire, where his mother, Fanny Levinson, had fled to avoid the Zeppelin
raids on London. His father, fur-cutter Barnet Bernstein, had moved to
London from Russia at the age of 13—a story so typical of the Jewish refugees
working in East London's 'rag trade'. The young Joe Bernstein lived with his
parents above a cobbler's shop in Hare Street, Bethnal Green, close to the vast
railway yards whose sights, sounds and smells dominated the youngster's
early years. He later wrote of his memory of how the outer walls of his home
were stained with soot from the railway engines and how the voices of the
carters carried into his home, as they moved through the cobbled streets.
Rather ominously, he noticed how these men all seemed to wear the remnants
of army uniforms, a mark of their service in the Great War.

Although it would eventually be the army that came to dominate his life,
during the 1930s Baron was drawn—as were so many of his generation—
into the world of left-wing politics. In 1934 he joined the Labour League of
Youth (the Labour Party's youth wing). As his contemporary in the LLOY,
and later wartime comrade, Harry Ratner wrote,

By 1936 the LLOY in London had become polarised into bitterly opposed Stalinist and Trotskyist factions with hardly any ordinary 'Labourites' in between. Any new members like myself joining were soon courted and recruited by the rival factions. The Trotskyists won me over but Bernstein/Baron must have been recruited by Ted Willis's 'Advance' faction, which seceded and joined the Young Communist League.

He soon became recognised as an active and important member of the Young Communists, meeting many leading figures within the movement. He and his comrades worked hard to fight back against the burgeoning fascist movement of Oswald Mosley and his 'Blackshirts'. Baron was also active in the movement to support the Spanish Government in its fight against Franco's rebel forces in the Spanish Civil War. It was to his eternal regret that the Communist Party believed him too important at home to be allowed to travel to Spain to fight for the cause.

Despite spending many hours reading what he later referred to as 'tedious texts' by Lenin and Stalin, Baron remained a party loyalist, something that was soon to be challenged in his experience of war. When war was declared, he went against the 'party line' and attempted to join the RAF, only to be turned down due to his poor eyesight. Yet he was undeterred—knowing that he wanted to fight the menace of Nazi Germany despite the thoughts of either the RAF recruiting officer or the leaders of the Communist Party. He later described the spark of character that provoked his defiance: 'Another self was always there, waiting its time.'

It was during the war years that this 'other self' began to emerge. Called up into the army, his poor eyesight meant that, following basic training, he was posted to the Pioneer Corps and served in 243 Company. Despite the initial stages of his drift away from the Communist Party, Baron continued outwardly to display his loyalty. He wrote for *Challenge*, the newspaper of the Young Communist League, and even recruited fellow soldiers to sell the newspaper among his company. Such were the strict dividing lines between the various elements of the British left that his communist activities forced him apart from a fellow veteran of the Labour League of Youth serving in 243 Company. Harry Ratner later recalled,

> I have no real memories of Joe Bernstein [Baron] because he was a Communist Party member. I had been in contact with him in the Labour League of Youth.

But I was a Trotskyist. Relationships between Stalinists and Trotskyists were very fraught. Their official line was that all Trotskyists were fascist agents.

He recalled the violent division between the two groups:

We used to run street-corner meetings opposite Whitechapel Hospital. One evening we would be attacked by the fascists, who told us 'Go back to Moscow,' the next day we would be attacked by the Communist Party, who said we were bloody fascists!

As Ratner remembered, there was no wartime reconciliation:

When I found out that there was a Joe Bernstein in my company, who had been in the Labour League of Youth in the East End of London, I didn't really want to get into an argument with him—and I don't think he wanted to get into an argument with me. So we kept a distance from each other. Now, looking back on it, I'm very sorry I didn't try to get into discussion with him because we might have found out we agreed more than we disagreed.

At one point Baron was chosen for officer training, passed the initial course, but did not receive a commission. Close attention had been paid to his communist activity and, it appeared, the decision had been taken that Baron was best left in the ranks. Instead he remained a labourer in the Pioneer Corps, whose myriad tasks included digging defensive positions, tunnelling, road building, clearing enemy defences, laying mines and generally carrying out 'pick and shovel' duties. Effectively, they were the 'muscle' of the army, who shed sweat and blood without sharing any of the glory. In the years that followed, Baron found that the 'womblike warmth of comradeship' began to replace his allegiance to the Communist Party.

Despite the seemingly mundane duties of the Pioneer Corps, war took Baron to Sicily, where he rowed ashore during the assault landings before spending weeks in the front line; Italy, where he again experienced the horrors of life in the front line; Normandy, where he landed on 'Gold Beach' and spent D-Day ferrying vehicles from ship to shore, often under fire; Mont Pinçon, where he witnessed the decimation of the 5th Battalion of the Wiltshire Regiment (which formed the basis for his first novel *From the City, From the Plough*); and Belgium, where he worked 19 hours a day in the docks at Antwerp and faced constant attack from V1 rockets. In more than a year of almost constant action, Baron and his comrades in 243 Company found themselves bringing up supplies to the front line, filling in bomb craters to allow roads to be used, clearing minefields and dismantling the enemy's defences—usually under incoming fire. And at the end of battle, it was Baron and his comrades who dug the graves for the dead.

In early 1945 he was sent to Northern Ireland for retraining, in preparation for a transfer to the infantry. It was there that Baron was involved in an accident with an army lorry, and the psychical effect of this then seemed to trigger a breakdown, a result of the tension that had built up inside him during the campaigns in Sicily, Italy, France and Belgium. As he later wrote, 'I felt that innumerable fine wires inside me were being tightened on violin pegs.' The breakdown—which left him feeling 'a bit humiliated about not being able to stand the pace'—hastened his discharge from the army, as noted on his release papers, due to 'Psychoneurosis...aggravated by war service, but not attributable thereto.'

Released from the army, Baron returned to London, supported himself by writing theatre reviews, and began work on the novel that would make him known worldwide. Written on a typewriter he had received upon demobilisation, Baron's novel—*From the City, From the Plough*—immediately caught the attention of publishers, being accepted by Jonathan Cape in August 1947: £50 advance on signature, £50 on publication. The first thing the publishers did was to request he changed his name, since Bernstein didn't fit comfortably onto the spine. They told him to choose a five-letter name, thus Alexander Baron was born. With this rebirth under a new name, Baron finally made the split from the Communist Party. In later years he remained friendly with many ex-comrades and, unlike some notable figures, he never denied his past political stance. However, his understanding of humanity—as learned in wartime—was too independent for his literature or thoughts ever again to be restrained by the 'party line'.

The book was published in May 1948, to both immediate acclaim and commercial success, the 3000-copy print run selling out even before publication. Readers were soon joined by reviewers, who heaped praise on Baron. In the words of V.S. Pritchett, *From the City, From the Plough* was 'The only war book that has conveyed any sense of reality to me.' The *Spectator* called it 'A small masterpiece'. The reviewer for the *People* made the highest comparison: 'I have found the war book that tells it all...We have waited a long time for this war's *All Quiet on the Western Front*. Here it is.' Most importantly, the *Star* recommended it to veterans: 'every reader who fought in Europe will acclaim his story as the real thing.'

A second novel, *There's No Home*, followed in 1950, and told the story of British soldiers resting in Catania during the Sicilian campaign. It was based on Baron's observations of his fellow soldiers and their interactions with the local civilian population. Two more novels followed (*Rosie Hogarth*, 1951, and *With Hope, Farewell*, 1952) and then, in 1953, *The Human Kind* was published. Baron considered it, along with *From the City, From the Plough* and *There's No Home*, to be the final part of a trilogy based on his wartime experiences: 'My three war books constitute a single body of work in which the broadening exploration of the theme can be seen.' He hoped a combined volume would one day be issued under the title *Men, Women and War,* and described the books as reflecting his 'cycle of experience'.

In his unpublished autobiography, Baron acknowledged the debt he owed to war, which gave him the necessary understanding of human nature to allow his writing to flourish. He admitted he had 'come into the army knowing nothing about people except what I had got from literature approved by the [Communist] Party as correct...My call-up was truly a release.' In *The Human Kind* he repaid that debt by painting a variety of literary portraits of the men he had served alongside. These characters were good and bad, sometimes both. More than anything, as advertised by the title, they were human. In effect, they were men who carried on with their own lives, in their own way, against a backdrop of war. As Harry Ratner noted, 'They didn't really have any opinion about the war. It was just something that happened. And they happened to be in it. And they had to make the best of it. Any loyalty they had was an immediate loyalty to their mates.' These were the types that Baron knew, respected, and whose lives and experiences he recorded for posterity. As with all of Baron's war books, he wrote not about heroes but about the everyday heroics of reluctant warriors.

Although written as a sequence of short stories, *The Human Kind* is effectively a series of vignettes—fictionalised episodes from his military service. It is part novel (in that the stories follow an identified, historical path), part memoir (in that it follows Baron's own experiences) and part collection of short stories (in that most of the stories can stand alone). The book does not identify its narrator, except towards the end, when he is referred to as 'Alex'. However, as he later wrote, 'I have written three books about the lives of men and women in the war. I made use in these books of my own experiences as well as of scenes that I witnessed and stories that others told me.' Despite the use of the name 'Alex', the narrator is not Baron, but a composite, an 'everyman' who reflects the good-natured, positive-thinking men that helped make Baron's wartime service such a defining experience. These were the men whose comradeship helped divert Baron's politics away from the hard line espoused by the Communist Party. As a communist he had idealised 'the working man', yet as a soldier he grew to love the ordinary men that he met, seeing them as fully rounded individuals rather than a romanticised, proletarian ideal. These are ordinary men who surprise Baron by their love of Dickens, Burns and Beethoven, not ignorant caricatures of the type portrayed in so many war novels, or the idealised working class of some left-wing writers.

The book begins with a seemingly unconnected tale, the story of a youth during the 1930s taking part in a cycle trip into the countryside as part of a large group of local teenagers. This opening sequence reflects the freedom of youth at an age when 'death is an impossibility'—a concept that was soon to be torn from the grasp of Baron's generation. In this introduction Baron constantly hints at the impending war: swimming in a river, the youths feel 'the tug of the current against our own strength' as it pulled them towards a weir that surely represents war. When the rains come, they appear as if from the gathering storm clouds of war. It is obvious but realistic, reflecting the world that Baron had inhabited—where youthful political activity had also provided an environment to meet girls (a theme developed in his 1971 novel *The In-between Time*). When the narrator falls from his bike and is injured, a cigarette is placed between his lips and he is handed a cup of hot, sweet tea. As Baron had witnessed so many times, this was exactly the initial treatment given to wounded men in wartime. In these opening pages Baron gives the reader a synopsis of his young life: bespectacled lad enjoys the freedom of youth, is dragged into a war, witnesses the 'storm of war' and is injured. But at the end he is ready to carry on with life.

The story follows the basic course of Baron's war: from the boredom and seeming futility of service in the UK, to Sicily, to Italy, on to France and the low countries. When necessary, he breaks away from the anonymity of a fictional narrator and reveals directly personal thoughts. At the end of a story about a bored sentry he reveals, 'That was what it felt like to be young and in uniform, in Britain, in the late summer of nineteen-forty.' In the middle of the book ('The Indian') the narration briefly ceases while Baron recounts the true story behind the central theme of his earlier novel *There's No Home*, revealing what really happened between its central characters. And then he returns to anonymity. Later he uses this anonymity to tell some of the most personal elements as an observer, rather than in the first person. One feels that, so soon after war's end, he was not yet ready to lay himself bare to his readership.

The short stories reveal so many elements of war: the futility of kindness, the dislocation of society, the collision of cultures and the cheapness of life. More than anything, Baron reveals the careful psychological balancing act of soldiers, between the callous disregard for humanity and their—at times— overwhelming appreciation of beauty, however small and insignificant. In Baron's world, good men grow hard and sullen, their manners and values changed, while quiet, seemingly inoffensive men grow embittered—however well they are treated.

In 'The Hunchback Woman' Baron shows the sexual ignorance of many of those of his generation, contrasting it with the antics of the older, more worldly wise men he served with. The story is loosely based on his own experiences and the tale of the relationship between a comrade and a local woman known as 'Black Bess'. Elsewhere in the book, Baron is not critical of the loose sexual morals of others, even though the reader is certain that Baron did not share their values. When he writes of Belgian brothels it is from direct experience and observation, rather than from participation.

In 'Old Beethoven' he describes what one might call 'the comradeship of shit': the often-ignored element of depersonalisation that takes place in every army as men learn to live together without embarrassment. In Baron's case it is the story of soldiers sharing a slit-trench, under gunfire, with one of them suffering from dysentery. In one of the most important chapters, 'The Pillbox', Baron makes reference to the Pioneer Corps and reveals how he and his comrades had so often been in the heart of the action. In this episode he reflects the lack of recognition they received for their work and how they were perceived by outsiders. More importantly, he admits to the degree to which war changed him as—in another aside—he reveals how for years after the war he told a tragic story as if it were a comedy, forgetting that the punchline revolved around tragically avoidable deaths.

There are many episodes within *The Human Kind* in which one can imagine Baron sitting in a dingy European café listening to soldiers talking, and unconsciously recording the stories in his memory, ready to be replayed in novel form. Once again he alludes to the sacrifices of the Wiltshire Regiment that he had witnessed in Normandy, and recounted in *From the City, From the Plough*, when he reveals one of the more sympathetic characters as being from Wiltshire. Though written from the perspective of the narrator, 'Victory Night' is perhaps the most personal of all the stories in the book. He recounts the story of 'Frank Chase'. Yet Chase is clearly Baron himself. It is a clear and concise portrait of the impact of war upon him. While his unpublished memoirs and personal letters give snippets of his experiences in the final months of war, it is this chapter that brings them all together to reveal starkly the true effect of all he had experienced. In a startling admission, Baron notes, 'Frank imagined himself born to put the world right by worrying.' It also admits to how 'political theories' had 'gripped him with the force of religious mania', but that he could no longer reconcile the dogma of his politics with the real world he saw around him. In this self-analysis, Baron is open about himself, critical of his naïvety, and honest in how he was haunted by dreams of war.

The success of the book—resulting in good reviews and good sales— brought further attention. The American film producer Carl Foreman— another former communist—acquired the rights to *The Human Kind*, with the film being released in 1963 under the title *The Victors*. However, what could have been a high point in Baron's career became one of his most bitter disappointments. In attempting to attract an American audience, Foreman rewrote the story, abandoned the British setting and made all the characters American. Very little of the original book remained, and Baron was upset by the changes, wanting his name removed from the credits. It was a bitter blow to a writer who had a very personal attachment to the men he had served with. He had reflected their lives and put so much of his own emotion into *The Human Kind* that he felt cheated.

Perhaps responding to this snub, Baron wrote a screenplay called *The Poor Bloody Infantry* that he hoped would restore the rightful place of the British soldier in the cinematic history of World War II. The story was based on a real incident in which a British platoon attacked a German-held farmhouse in Belgium in late 1944. For Baron, the most important thing was to create a sense of authenticity: 'It is a lack of realism in detail which has spoiled British war films so far.' He wanted a director to look at the way soldiers move on the battlefield and recreate that. He wanted to show the dead and wounded in realistic detail. He even wanted the actors to be taught period battle drill to ensure they moved correctly, 'not just run fiercely about'. Explosions should be realistic, not just puffs of smoke. In the conclusion of his proposal for the film he revealed the very essence of his memory of war: 'the keynote of this— I've never seen any film before that portrayed this—is suspense, not knowing, and waiting. Waiting, waiting, waiting, that is the real strain of war.'

Baron had captured this in *The Human Kind*, been cheated out of seeing it in cinemas with *The Victors*, and attempted—without success—to rectify this with *The Poor Bloody Infantry*. So for any filmmakers out there, the rights are still available...

London, 2011

The Human Kind

Strangers to Death:
A Prologue

When I was sixteen my parents bought me a bicycle. It was a sports model, with cream mudguards and handlebars, light blue frame and chromed fittings: the most beautiful work of art I had yet encountered.

I had been worshipping it for weeks in its shop window, and pleading with my parents for it. They had resisted, not because it was expensive but because it was dangerous. They had weakened, and offered to buy me a cheap, safe machine. Then they had come with me to the shop, seen me looking at the 'Silver Wing' and—as working-people generally do for their children—they had bought it for me.

I had never ridden a full-size bicycle before. The older boys in the street, owners of machines even more graceful and expensive than mine, would not take the risk of giving rides to a beginner. I brought my 'Silver Wing' home on a Friday, promised my parents that I would not go out of the street with it until I was sufficiently practised, spent the evening wobbling round and round the block on it—and the next morning I set off on a weekend trip.

Every Saturday morning from early spring to late autumn, a crowd of young people would meet at the street corner. The cyclists, with rucksacks on their backs, tin mugs and kettles, all a-rattle, tied with string to their crossbars, and cheap little tents slung under the saddles, would stream away along the Cambridge road to their camping-site by the River Lea. Others would follow by bus.

On Saturday morning, then, I carried my bicycle down the front steps into the lovely May sunshine with happiness racing inside me, and a rucksack and brew-kettle on my back, and joined the group at the street corner.

This was a rash thing to do, for the weekly swoop out of town was led by a group of veterans who set a furious pace, heading a follow-my-leader at top speed in and out of the traffic that was beyond the skill of a beginner.

However, I set off with the others, frightened, excited and filled with a blissful lightness of spirit. How miraculous it seemed, for the first few minutes, to feel the bicycle riding easily underneath me, the pedals driving springily beneath my toecaps, the road surface streaming towards me! How easy it suddenly seemed! How quickly confidence was born, and how quickly it gave birth, in its turn, to boyish vainglory! I was an aviator, riding in one of the echelons of his squadron. I was a cavalryman in the ranks of his thundering troop.

Gradually, as the legs of the riders became accustomed to the rhythm of pedalling, the leaders increased the pace. To keep my place in the line, I had to ride as hard as I could, throwing all my weight down upon my calf muscles, driving my legs like pistons. My head was bent low over the handlebars. All I could see was my own front tyre, spinning, spinning, and hissing as the pattern of roadblocks came reeling back to meet it; and the vibrating rear mudguard of the machine in front of me.

This was the point at which, in the wakeful night before, I had feared difficulties, panic, accident or a defeated dropping-out of the line. But nothing went wrong. There was no ache in my legs. I felt them flying beneath me like birds. I was aware of nothing except that mudguard in front of me, always to be followed, and in pursuit of it I plugged uphill, raced downhill, sliding past traffic lights as they changed, weaving among vehicles, shooting through the narrow slots of space between halted trucks and buses.

Thought, knowledge, would have meant disaster. But at sixteen, death is an impossibility, therefore danger has no imaginable consequences, and is only a stimulant, to be taken as often as possible. I rode on, so fast that my bewildered mind was left behind, and all I knew was the song that the purring chain sang to me, vanity, vanity, vanity, vanity...

Once I skidded on an oil-patch. The machine whirled round under me. I had no idea what was happening. Other bicycles swerved outwards to avoid me, shot past and closed their ranks in front of me. A second later I realised that I had ridden through the skid and was pedalling safely on. My body, too young to have been spoiled by experience, had made all the correct adjustments before my mind knew what had happened. It swayed to right or left as the fleeting moment demanded. My unskilled hands squeezed and relaxed on the brakes, guided the handlebars to swerve and straighten the machine, always sure and precise, disconnected from the brain. Inwardly I was aware, simultaneously, of growing fright and of growing fearlessness—and of nothing else in my whole being.

We camped about twenty miles north of London, under the hedge in a field by the river bank. We lay about all day, cooked meals on Primus stoves and spent the evening in a nearby pub.

It was very hot on the Sunday morning and we went swimming. The boys in their bathing-trunks and the girls in their tight, brightly coloured costumes leaped and pranced on the pebbles of the towpath, with exaggerated yelps of pain, and shot into the water with short, flashing dives.

We loved to swim in this part of the river, for there was a weir a little way downstream. Where we dived in, the current was already gathering speed, but we could still swim easily against it. The farther we swam downstream, the more powerful the current became, and the harder it was to swim back against it; until the water, hardening into a green, grooved, glassy compactness, slid over the edge of the weir to crash below in an incessant thunder of white foam.

What could be more attractive, then, than to slip downstream with the current, and to see how far we could dare to go before we turned to swim back? It was frightening, and maddening, to feel the tug of the current against our own strength, and to hear the thundering fall of water. We felt fear piercing us, and we swam back out of its reach. Our strength prevailed, and because we thought that it must always prevail, we remembered the stab of fear only as a sensual pleasure.

Towards midday, when it was so hot that we dried as soon as we climbed out of the water, and we could feel the sun's burning touch on our bare bodies, shouts attracted our attention from farther along the river bank. A crowd of bathers had collected, and we went to see what was the matter.

A boy had been drowned. We knew him. He camped in the same field as us and he came from the same district. He had been caught by the silkweed.

The silkweed floated beneath the surface of the river, green, grassy tresses thirty feet long, undulating in the current with a siren languor. An old boatman, standing over the dead boy, sweating after his vain attempts to bring back respiration, told us that it was fatal to be caught in the silkweed. It was impossible to break the strands when they wrapped themselves around the body. The more one struggled, he said, the more the disturbed water would bind them round their victim.

We watched an ambulance take the boy's body away, feeling nothing except embarrassment. We wandered back along the towpath, awkwardly, because we felt that we ought to keep quiet, at least for a little while, and we did not want to keep quiet. Our spirits were not subdued, only cramped. The fact of his death meant nothing to us. A face that we had seen in the field was no longer there: that was all.

We had our lunch quietly and rested afterwards. Later in the afternoon, when it was already growing cool, we began to stir and look expectantly at each other, feeling that we had remained quiet long enough for the sake of someone who wasn't even alive. We went back to the river, running to warm ourselves against the eddies of cold wind that roughened our skin.

One by one the swimmers flashed into the river like diving birds, came up to the surface, each in a boil of white water, and struck out. As they felt the shock of the cold water they shouted wildly, and thrashed with their arms and legs until the air over the river echoed once more with a tumult of young voices and the noise of churned water.

The drowning of the boy had suggested to us an exciting new game—to play with the silkweed.

Swimming under water, I saw my companions come floating down one by one, slipping sinuously underneath me or passing me slowly with flexing limbs. Some of them rolled playfully over me, dark shadows above cutting off the light, then, quick as minnows, darting away down into the green subaqueous gloom, leaving little clusters of bubbles behind.

And there, among the waving weeds, we played, heading down through the midst of the weed, seeing it part respectfully (moved by the ripples we made with our outstretched hands) to make a path for us, running it through our fingers, winding it round our arms, tugging at it, disturbing it with our legs. Up to the surface, bursting out into the cold white daylight, taking in a deep lungful of air and somersaulting forward, bottom upward, to go down again, into the kingdom of the long, green, undulating weeds.

The air grew chill and the lustre faded from the light. We went back to our field and dressed. We cooked a last meal, lay smoking in our tents for a couple of hours while the shadows and deep colours of evening gathered in the sky, then we struck the tents and packed our rucksacks.

Dusk invaded the fields. The hedgerows loomed black behind us, the river, glimpsed through gently stirring foliage, was a deep olive surface, with scarcely a gleam of white light upon it. It might have been still water but for the deep, sluicing sound of its flow.

A first party left us: girls, who would go back to town by bus. Soon after, a second group went away: all those girls and boys who had slow upright bicycles. The owners of racing machines, 'the high-speed flight', stayed behind. I stayed with them. I was tired in body and spirit. I was reluctant to face any more tests, and my confidence was ebbing, but I had to go through to the end of this day of initiation. And my machine stood behind me, against the hedge, too beautiful for me to disgrace it.

It was dark now. The riders stubbed out their cigarettes and moved quietly about in the long grass, strapping gear to their carriers. When they spoke, their voices were muffled by the darkness. They set out across the field, a long single line of dark figures wheeling their bicycles silently beside them. To me they looked like cavalrymen leading their mounts to some fateful point of assembly. They came to the gate and, disdaining to open it, they lifted their bicycles easily over it, one by one. My turn came. I strained with all my strength and heaved the machine over the gate, clambering after it.

We came out on to the road, switched on our headlamps, mounted and rode away in a double line. We climbed a hill, pedalling with slow, hard strokes that brought warmth and an ache that would soon pass. Riding more easily, we topped the hill and swerved out on to the arterial road, the broad straight highway that cut through patterns of fields and warrens of suburbs into London.

And now something I had not foreseen happened. It began to rain. A thin slanting drizzle prickled coldly upon our faces. A treacherous film of rain formed upon the road surface, gleaming blackly. Cars shot past us, one after another, each with an intimidating swish, buffeting us with their wind, a stream of shadowy projectiles that crowded us in to the verge and swept the wet surface with silent swathes of yellow. Our column gained speed. There was nothing I could do but keep my place in the line, pedalling faster and faster, flying along without feeling the ground beneath me, as if I were airborne in a black cloudland.

My glasses were wet, and all I could see was a world of flashing, shifting stars. In the middle of this world winked the red rear reflector of the machine in front of me. I lost all notion of where I was, or where I was going. All I knew was to keep my headlamp shining on that little red guide, and to flee from the hissing menace of the machine behind me.

We rode, rode, down the long tunnel of darkness, knees shuttling, all to one rhythm. My pedals were flashing round and round as if a machine drove them. It was no longer my feet which impelled them but they which whirled my feet (held by the rattrap grips) over and over at a runaway pace. The machine was my master. The journey was years long. I had lost track of its beginning and could not conceive that it would end. Blinded by my wet glasses I swooped on through the stars and spears of light. The cold, wet wind on my face numbed my senses and its soft roar, blustering in my ears, cut me off from the voices of my companions and the sounds of the real, surrounding world.

At last we were coming into town. The tension slackened, and with it my blind will slackened, so that I was now able to think, to fear, to hesitate. The road narrowed. On each side were brilliantly lit shops, neon-lit cinemas, pavements overflowing with crowds, people darting across in our path, great red buses lumbering in front of us.

The pace slowed, but the steady, flowing regularity of the column continued. We were riding on fat, treacherous cobblestones, on a wet road that sloped in a steep camber to the gutters. On our right ran tramlines, deep metal slots, slippery with rain, that waited to trap our narrow tyres and fling the riders under some rumbling truck.

To my seniors, the tramlines were a final happy challenge. Buses, stopping and starting, blocked the narrow carriageway in front of us. As the line of riders came up behind each bus, they did not slow down to let it move away in front of them, but swerved out, at undiminished speed, on to the tramlines. One by one the machines shot round each stationary bus and swung back into line in front of it, and each time each rider had to make in an eye's blink a series of precise calculations and movements. He had to swing over the outer tramline at a sharp enough angle to prevent his front tyre from slipping into the slot. He had to straighten out, on a foot-wide strip of greasy cobbles, before he hit the middle line; then swing back over the outer rail again.

Time after time they did this, and time after time I rode with them, blind now with fright, but travelling too fast, trapped in my place in line, to drop out. It was raining harder. I could see nothing at all through the blurred circles of my lenses, except the red light in front of me. All confidence gone, lost in nightmare, I rode on and waited for the fall.

The last hill confronted us, and the last swoop down into our own High Street. The lights were brighter, the crowds more dense than ever. We came over the hill and rode down the last slope. A bus loomed in front of us. The line of bicycles in front of me swerved out on to the tramlines. I swerved with it, sped alongside the bus, swung to the left in front of the bus.

There was a wild, incredulous second when I felt myself turning over in the air, still feeling the leap the machine had given beneath me, the sickening sensation as it slewed away from under me. I hit the roadway and rolled to the left. I was aware of the bus moving forward, enormous above me, its headlamps shining down at me. I heard the screams of women.

I rolled into the gutter and the bus lumbered past. I climbed to my feet, feeling stupid and lazy. People were gathering around me, their faces and voices hostile, all of them telling me what I deserved to be told. I could not take in what they were saying. I stared out across the road. I was full of anxiety for my bicycle. There it lay, across the tramlines, with car after car steering clear of it.

The bus had stopped a little way down the road, and the driver came back. He was a big, heavy man, his face engraved with the cares of his work and his family. Fright had made him angry, and he lectured me in a deep, stern voice. I stood like a sheep, unable to answer.

My friends had ridden on, most of them probably unaware of what had happened. The two men behind me, both of whom had displayed the skill of trick riders in avoiding my spill, had dismounted and came walking back, with a slow, accusing step. They asked me if I felt all right. I looked at them in a daze and said, 'My bike?'

We went to look at it. It was undamaged. The front wheel was not twisted by the wrench the slot had given it. Even the headlamp was still burning. One of my friends said, 'You're a lucky one,' and handed my glasses to me. They had been flung into the kerb by the force of my fall, but they were not broken.

We remounted. For the first few seconds as I rode, my legs shook. Then confidence came back, and the pleasure of riding, and we glided down the road to the Italian café that was our destination.

We went in. I felt no ill-effects except a warm, drowsy sensation in my right leg. We stacked our bicycles with the others against the wall and sat down at marble-topped tables. Jacko, the proprietor, was drawing tea from a big urn, and hurrying to and fro to serve us. The room was very warm. My glasses steamed up, and I had to take them off. The electric light dazzled me, and I felt slightly sick.

Everyone gathered round me, and I realised with joy that I had not only come through this first ride, but had become a person of importance.

I moved my right leg, and the warm numbness became damp. I put my right hand down, lifted it up, and saw four finger-tips brightly touched with blood. I put my foot up on another chair, undid the straps of my cycling-breeches, and the blood (which had already stained the tweed from knee to ankle) ran out.

There was a great fuss. Jacko called to his wife. She rushed in with a bowl of hot water. One of the boys found a dressing in his saddlebag. My leg was washed, painted with iodine and bandaged. Everyone crowded round. The girls were wide-eyed, I was happy, proud of the blood, asking with swaggering calm for a cigarette, which somebody put between my lips as if he was proud to be involved. Jacko asked me if I wanted to go along to the hospital and I, imitating the manner of my seniors, answered, 'Nah, I'm all right.'

I asked Jacko to bring me a nice, hot cup of tea, with plenty of sugar, and I spent the next half-hour explaining in voluble detail what had happened.

At midnight, the group broke up. Boys and girls paired off and went away, wheeling their bicycles, to hide away for an hour in their secret corners—dark doorway, back alley, park bench or front parlour—before they parted.

A little girl of my own age said to me (in our youthful community the girls were quite guileless in their overtures), 'Can I walk home with you?'

I answered, 'OK, Kath,' and we walked out together. I limped exaggeratedly, and we both held the handlebars of my bicycle as it purred along on the pavement between us.

The night was warm. We were happy. We talked about next weekend, and the next summer holidays, a time that seemed infinitely distant. Life was inexhaustible and death was still beyond our ken.

The Sentry

I remember a night, towards the end of August, nineteen-forty. A sentry was pacing up and down his beat outside an Army barracks in Southampton. The building, a requisitioned school, was surrounded by a high brick wall, and the sentry's beat lay along the pavement outside this wall, from a sandbagged dugout at the gate to the street corner.

He marched with a grave, rigid step, his rifle held faultlessly at the slope, his straight right arm swinging up to shoulder level and down to his side in harmony with each pace. At the corner, where his beat met that of the next man, he halted and went through the motions of the about-turn, his knees coming up high as if a drill sergeant were watching him, the steel tips of his boots crashing on the pavement with machine-like regularity—one, two, three, four and away again—marching stiffly back along his beat.

Why was he marching with such punctilio? There was no one to see him. The street was dark and deserted. Nor was there any need for him to march. For at this moment an air-raid was at its height. His orders permitted him to take cover in the dugout whenever bombers were overhead. They were, without any doubt, overhead now. Their savage, uneven roar filled his ears. The air was alive with the transient whistle and flutter of falling bombs. The rolling thud of explosions could be heard from every direction and from time to time all other sounds were engulfed by the clifflike fall, prolonged and awe-inspiring, of some large building. On the other side of the wide green which the sentry's beat overlooked, a black row of buildings was thrown into relief by the glow of distant fires, sometimes faint, sometimes waxing into a bright, enormous glare. Anti-aircraft batteries ripped and slammed. One group of guns, dug in on the green only a couple of hundred yards away, shook the night with a deafening outburst each time the bombers passed overhead.

It was unnecessary for him to march. It was foolish for him to march. Perhaps he was weak in the head; but if so, he was not the only one; for at each of the two limits of his beat, another sentry always marched to meet him, and each of the other two men matched him in stiffness of carriage and unhurrying regularity of step. As he halted, the other man would halt. Neither of them would speak. There would only be a mutual amused scrutiny of the eyes. He would turn about, hearing the other man turning in time with him—crash, crash, crash, crash and away again—and the other man's steps would fade along the far beat in time with his own. And all about them the storm roared, the gunflashes split the darkness and the ambulance bells pierced it all with their racing clamour.

The sentry had only been in the Army for a few weeks. The transformation in his life had been so rapid that he had not yet caught up with it. Nothing seemed real to him any more. There had been the early summer, the most serene and lovely he could remember, and he had been courting a girl. There had been days at Richmond—his memory was full of the cool green smell of water, the ripple at the boat's bows, the shimmering translucent gloom, full of dancing sunbeams, beneath the gunwales, the soft burning touch of the sun, the dazzling empty glare of the sky, and the weight of the girl upon his shoulder. Bad news had been a distant, disbelieved babble.

Dunkirk had not broken the languid, light-filled spell. There was no feeling of danger; not as much suspense as in the last five minutes of an undecided football match. There was merely something to talk about. The mood—and this perhaps was the key to the whole of that strange time—was one of fascinated incredulity. Everybody waited to see how the film was going to end. One radiant summer day succeeded another, to heighten the illusion of holiday.

But one day, coming away from his girl, the young man stood on a railway platform. A train trundled past, and in its windows crowded bareheaded, sunburned men in uniform, staring at the world with the hungry curiosity of survivors. A hospital train followed, running through the station with a subdued clatter. He walked home, oppressed by confused thoughts. Two days later his calling-up papers came. His heart missed a beat; then he was filled with relief.

And now here he was, marching up and down in the middle of an air-raid like a toy soldier. He did this without thought, and if he had been asked why he did it, he would not have been able to answer. He came to the sandbagged sentry post at the gate. His neighbouring sentry arrived at the same moment. They halted, turned to their front, stepped a pace backwards, brought their arms ceremonially to the ground and stood stiffly at ease. Even now they did not turn their heads to talk, but looked straight to the front with empty, contented eyes.

They both listened—and each was aware of the other's tension—as one falling whistle grew unusually shrill and prolonged. In a common animal impulse they hurled themselves for the dugout entrance, and were writhing past each other into the comforting dark when a terrible white light filled their eyes, the pavement rocked and a detonation beat down upon them. Amid the ringing, remote echoes that filled their eardrums they heard the crack and tinkle of blasted windows. They both laughed, uneasily, at the near miss, and emerged on to the pavement. As they took up their positions again, the sentry said, his voice still a little shaken, 'He's a trier, old Jerry. He doesn't give up.'

The other man answered, 'Don't you worry. He'll get tired of it.' When they had rested for a few minutes, the other man said, 'OK?' They stepped forward together, sloped arms together, turned back to back and marched away, arms swinging high, along their beats.

His papers had arrived, and a week later a recruit train had whisked him away from life. He had let them shepherd him, one of a crowd, into camp. He had clothed his body in the uniform they had given him. Later, he had looked at himself wonderingly in a shop window, incredulous at what he saw. His mind was still away back in the summer's dream. It had not yet caught up with his conscripted body.

Yet something sustained him. He was happy, eager, fanatically keen. There was no martial spirit in him. He was innocent of any desire to get at the throats of the enemy. It was doubtful if he had any clear picture of an enemy in his mind. Armed with a petrol bottle, ten rounds of ammunition and an antique American rifle, he waited for an invader, but the coming of an invader was beyond his imagination. Fascinated incredulity. Where, then, did his excitement come from—the blissful, clear-headed intoxication inside him that bore him along?

It was evident that the same feeling pervaded his comrades. For this mob of lounging, undisciplined Cockneys, who liked their clothes to be gorgeous and their hair long at the neck, had all gone soldiering-mad. They were enthusiastic to a degree that confounded their superiors. When the quartermaster had been unable to get slings and cleaning materials for their rifles, they had gone to gunsmiths' shops and bought their own. They invaded bookshops in search of pamphlets about the rifle, the Lewis gun (then still in use) and the grenade. They stayed in their barrack rooms at night to practise loading with dummy cartridges and to test each other with the aiming disc.

Their superannuated rifles were coddled like dainty darlings. They cleaned them day and night. Despite the protests of their exasperated NCOs, they endlessly and needlessly polished the woodwork with furniture wax. Some of the men nearly ruined their rifles by cleaning the bolts—which had been stained to prevent them from reflecting sunlight—with emery paper. The company commander had to threaten court martial before he could stamp out the practice. They even competed—how incredible this would seem in a year's time!—to be picked for guard duty, and when a platoon supplied a guard, everyone in the room would combine to clean the equipment of the chosen men and send them out on parade like mannequins.

Why? Why? Perhaps it was the sudden and total disruption of their lives, the vanishing of the whole accustomed pattern, so that they found themselves miraculously released from all responsibility, free to fulfil the dream of being schoolboys again. Perhaps it was the incredible disappearance of the future that had created their present mindless and exalted mood. Was it the first taste of being in something, in a great stream, with others that aroused them? Or were deeper forces, which they could not consciously recognise, at work in them to engender the feeling of nationhood?

Consider, for instance, the happy-go-lucky indifference with which they accepted the air-raids. They had marched into this town, on a sunny afternoon, in the middle of a raid. They had made their way along a main street, a single file on each side of the road, while overhead groups of little silver Messerschmitts sped to and fro along the balloon barrage with blasting machineguns. One by one the balloons had subsided, crumpled and burning, to the earth, and the marching men had looked up, without fear because there was no recognition of danger, counting as the balloons—one, two, three, four, five, six—came down boiling in red flame beneath black pillars of smoke. The Heinkels had followed, in wide formations that stretched across the sky; and again, as the bombs fell, the men were too busy counting the massed squadrons to remember that their falling missiles were lethal. Since then the raids had been continuous—once there were nineteen in a day—and still the soldiers were unperturbed, because it was unbelievable that England should be bombed, and even while it was happening they could not believe it.

The sentry continued along his beat. A fire-engine raced past. A bomb fell nearby and a great white glare rose over the treetops. Along the other side of the road, by the green, a policeman came strolling on his beat. He wore a steel helmet, but otherwise he might have been whiling away a weary spell of duty on a peaceful summer night. He walked with the slow, heavy, everlasting step of all English policemen. He saw the sentry, and his hand came up in a friendly wave. The sentry waved back with his free hand.

The policeman walked on, and the sentry continued his patrol, smiling. He felt warm and happy at the sight of the policeman carrying on. It was not foolish, it was not unnecessary, to be unshaken. It was good to hear the ring of one's own boots on the pavement in the midst of this lethal din. It was good to see the policeman walking by and to know that he, too, might be heartened by the sight of a sentry stamping imperturbably up and down along his beat. Everything was going on. The bombs came crashing down, great buildings were tumbling into rubble, fires were burning against the darkness, but the firm tread of life could not be halted.

That was what it felt like to be young and in uniform, in Britain, in the late summer of nineteen-forty.

Copperfield and the 'Erbs

At the beginning of nineteen-forty-one the long wait set in: the years that passed like a vague dream, in which we forgot the world and thought ourselves forgotten by it, alone in our little clusters of Nissen huts on wide, deserted moors.

The dream flickered and changed: the days slipped away from us in fits and starts of training, as pleasant and divorced in our thoughts from any deadly purpose as games: the nights slipped away in long, lethargic guards or in sociable intercourse around the red-hot stoves. Gales roared about our ears, deafening us to the life of distant cities. Buffeted and aroused by them, free in the open air for the first time in our lives, we tasted the animal joy of living, glutting ourselves with physical exertions, enormous meals and deep, satisfying sleep.

In our huts we had time to talk, to play cards, to listen to the radio—those were the great days of Vera Lynn and Itma—and to read. It was then, in my twenty-third year, that I read for the first time in my life an English novel of any importance, *David Copperfield*.

My hut mates were nearly all Londoners, drawn from comparatively skilled occupations: a printer, a garage mechanic, some cabinet-makers and bricklayers, an electrician, a radio handyman. There was a fireman and a waiter from a West End hotel. They were a tough, turbulent crowd who referred to themselves as 'proper 'erbs', eagerly disciplined when they were on duty but at all other times conscious of the trade-union cards in their wallets. The officers, who at that time were conscientious and for the most part kindly reservists of the old school, were bewildered by a succession of protest meetings against burned stew, sit-down strikes against unpopular fatigues and deputations to protest against wet straw in the palliasses. Intelligently, the commanding officer encouraged his men to elect a welfare committee and thus cope with their own discomforts. His sergeant-major, who wore nineteen-fourteen ribbons, went about muttering, 'What an army! What a war!'

My comrades had little education, but they possessed a keen and hungry intelligence. At nights, in their debates, they leaped at the novel opportunity to explore other people's minds and to learn to express their own. I remember one typical occasion. For hours, until after midnight, we had been arguing whether socialism was against human nature. The lights had been switched off. One by one the men had fallen silent until only a corporal and I were at it, both of us tired but still doggedly belabouring each other with words from opposite ends of the hut. Both of us were, in a way, spokesmen for all the men; I, naively, for their hopes, the corporal, a Welsh cynic who knew how to draw a laugh, for all their disillusioning experiences. Between us, the men lay silently in their beds, thinking, open-eyed in the darkness, each man's wakefulness marked by the red spark of a cigarette-end. Another hour passed. All the cigarettes had gone out. The blackness and the silence lay heavily upon us. The two of us were still talking. The corporal, from his end of the hut, called to me, 'We've talked 'em all to sleep, boy. Better turn in.' At once, from all parts of the hut, the silence was broken by cries of dissent. 'No, carry on!' 'We're awake.' 'Go on, lads, we're listening.' The room was filled with the scuffle of men turning over in their blankets and the scratch and flare of matches as the cigarettes began to glow once more.

Copperfield came into my hands as the least unpromising of a batch of books given to us by the Women's Voluntary Services. It was an old edition, in tiny print that hurt my eyes, and it smelt vaguely of meals eaten over it. I was ill at the time, and stayed behind in the hut each day as billet orderly. I glanced through the pages without enthusiasm. I had read a lot of history and political literature, everything in the French language that I could lay my hands on, and enough thrillers and Books of the Month to stock a public library, but it had never occurred to me—or to anyone I knew—to read any of the great English novels.

The book worked on me like a religious conversion. I avoided people until I had finished it. I went to bed early every night, turned my back on my friends, made a tent of my blankets to shut out their conversation, and read by the light of an electric torch until my eyes were bursting with pain. I wandered about the camp hating Mr. Murdstone, or as exasperated with poor Dora Copperfield as if I had married her myself. I had imaginary conversations with Dickens about the book. I slipped away from fatigue parties and hid myself in the coal store with it. I could not bear to leave it, and at the same time I was filled with dread as I came nearer to the end, when there would be no more to read; and when I had finished, I was quite exhausted.

By this time several of my friends were waiting to borrow the book. My sudden withdrawal from the accustomed round of card schools, arguments and horse-play had inevitably aroused inquiry. To anyone who approached me I had nothing to say except an irritated, 'Oh, shove off!' They discussed the mysterious book among themselves. Somebody would ask me if there was plenty of action in it. Somebody else would comment that it must be 'a hot one'. Those who had heard of it pointed out that it was 'only a school book', but this failed to extinguish the curiosity.

After I had passed the book on to the next man, I was too busy sorting out my inner confusion of thought and excitement to be able to talk coherently about it. If anyone asked me about it I would answer, 'Why don't you read it yourself?'

A third man read it, and a fourth; and now, as the book went from bed to bed, a new subject crept into our midnight debates: *David Copperfield*.

'Here—' This was a typical remark. 'You know the bit that bloody nigh made me cry? Where David's mother dies.'

'Ah,' another man would say. 'I'll tell you the bit that got me—'

And all these great, cheerful young louts would compete, in a hubbub of interruptions, to confess without any shame which parts of the book had reduced them to tears. I doubt if more than a few hours of our waking time passed, in the next couple of months, without our giving some sign of the book's presence in our midst. A command from an NCO would produce the muttered reply, 'Barkis is willing'. A standard catch-phrase among us was, 'Your very 'umble servant'. Nobody was surprised if, in the course of the evening, a soldier lying across his bed with the book suddenly burst into great howls of laughter, rolling about and kicking his feet with delight as he gasped, 'Here, this geezer Micawber! Listen to this bit—'

One night, two men nearly came to blows over the book.

Some of us were in bed, the rest undressing, when one of the men said, 'I reckon that chap Steerforth's a right bastard. Mucking about with a kid like little Em'ly!'

From one of his comrades there came a wail of, 'Here, don't spoil it. I'm not up to that bit yet.'

Ignoring the interruption, other men joined in the discussion. Somebody said, 'You'd do the same if you had the chance.'

'What, me? With a poor sweet little kid like that?'

'Well, it's human nature, ain't it? Look at Steerforth. You wouldn't call him a bad bloke, would you?'

'He's spoiled, that's his trouble. It's always the same with rich people. Anything they want, they lay their hands on. They're used to it from the cradle. They don't stop to think of the harm they're doing. And I'll thank you not to class me with a feller like that, if you don't mind.'

'I'll class you with who I like. I know you, Bert Blain, and you've done worse than him in your time.'

It was at this point that the corporal had to step in between the two men.

I cannot remember anything before or since that acted on the lives of this group of men like *Copperfield*. The book ceased to be an entertainment. It became a passionate experience shared by all of them, revealing in them all their simplicity, their sentimentality and their dazzling, childlike capacity for belief. While they were reading the book it became reality to them, more sharply stamped on their consciousness than the real life that they were dreaming. Its characters were accepted as living people, to be admired or censured, and their example, enacted in our midst, a source—does this sound comical to the worldly-wise?—of moral revelation.

In time they forgot *David Copperfield*. I cannot record that it led them on to other books. They went back to their talk, their cards, to Vera Lynn and the pictures, the Sunday newspapers, the film weeklies and the pulp novelettes about murderers who cackled with maniac satisfaction while they slit their victims' stomachs.

As for me, I shall never forget it, not only for what it taught me about the real character of my comrades, but because it showed me what a novel ought to be. It seems to me that if all the novels of the present century were melted into one, they could not equal in achievement a single book by a writer who can induce in multitudes a miraculous belief in his visions, who uses his power to teach, who can reach across time even to the unlettered, and who can bring them into communion with each other and with him.

The Hunchback Woman

I am a small man; but when I stood, head, shoulders and chest, above the hunchbacked woman, I felt like a giant.

She lived alone in a little bungalow at the end of a row of cottages in which we were billeted. The village was a mile away. Around us stretched the Hampshire plain: parklands, woods, cornfields, gleaming watercress beds and meadows in which fat cattle stood like enamelled toys. To the north rose the enclosing rim of the Berkshire Downs. When the sun shone we seemed to be living in a vast bowl filled with golden light.

We were a small detachment, left to our own devices except for the visits that the company commander made once or twice a week to inspect or to pay us. It was often like this in the early days, when units were dispersed over wide areas with little to do. We trained desultorily in a field opposite our billets. We enjoyed the drill, the morning run, the occasional undisciplined route march, as if they were children's games. Indeed, to us they were, for most of us had been scooped up into the army from the London streets where, still in our 'teens or early twenties, we had passed our time lounging or playing leapfrog or kicking footballs about like the overgrown children that Cockneys still are at an age when young people of a different class, at college or in a profession, are already swimming against the complex currents of adult life. We noticed little and learned little of the country life around us, but for all that we were vaguely delighted by the enormous vistas of cloud and sky, by a new vision of ourselves as tiny creatures in a universe of light, by the sweet taste of the air, the unending liquid thrill of birdsong and the harmony of bright but gentle colours. For the first time in our lives we knew what it was to be unenclosed, and the sensation of freedom enchanted us, even though we did not know what it was. Strolling, we would stop to watch a shaggy-maned old horse galloping round a field, or a ripple passing across the corn, or a sudden wild waving of treetops in a gust of evening breeze. Life had never been so calm for any of us. We sunbathed, sat on the white fence by the pond and watched the ducks, walked the lanes with our pockets full of stolen apples, and were happy.

Every day the hunchbacked woman, going to work in the village, toiled past us on her bicycle. It was small, but it was too big for her, and she had to throw herself forward on the pedals with all her puny weight so that the machine, scarcely controlled, lurched to and fro across the narrow lane. Sometimes she stopped at our cookhouse, to leave a basket of fruit for us, or some eggs. I talked with her several times. She was only about thirty, with a fragile flushed face that I would have thought pretty above another body, and pitifully thin limbs. It was embarrassing to talk to her. She was shy, always displaying a rigid smile, talking in a stifled polite voice, subjecting me all the time to a fixed, appealing stare with her big clear eyes, and often blushing suddenly for no reason that I could understand. Young though she was, I saw an old woman when I looked at her; but I could not help talking to her as I would to a child.

I envied Ted Trower, our driver, who was seldom on duty and often had time to talk to her, for the easy and natural way in which he was able to behave with her. I envied him, as I had on other occasions, because he was a man of the world compared with the rest of us, the only one of us who was equal to any human encounter that might befall him. He had been a travelling showman before the war, and at twenty-five he had seen most of the British Isles. He was slender, dark-haired and stooping. When I first saw him I labelled him as a corner-boy; then I saw his eyes, hot, piercing, authoritative, full of bitter wisdom; and I forgot his slouch. He could talk at length without seeming loquacious; his voice was always low, ironic, faintly tired. When he told us of his adventures with a flea circus, with a race gang, with tramps, women, buskers, pedlars, policemen, fairground bruisers, we always believed him although often he was openly exercising his gift for invention. We would roar with laughter, for his tales were funny and fantastic, but his tone would never vary, never gaining in animation yet never losing its even strength. He would heap one monstrosity upon another, watching us all the time with an expression of grave mockery as if he were making scientific tests of our credulity. Occasionally, at our request, he would stand on a table and act the sideshow barker for us. Then he would become a different person, loud, jovial, hectoring. If we had seen him only in this role we would never have guessed at his other personality.

Whenever the little hunchback came he would appear in another character altogether, and this, too, was as unforced and consistent as if it were his only self. He would be boyish, friendly, his face alive with pleasure at seeing her. He would talk to her gently, without the condescension that we others could not avoid showing. He would ask her to wash a shirt for him, or to stew a rabbit that he had caught; although nobody else liked to ask her for favours, he knew how happy any such occupation made her. Instead of keeping carefully to conventional topics of conversation as the rest of us did, he would ask her blunt questions about her life which, so far from hurting her, elicited eager replies; and he would tell her—this respectable little church mouse—some of his coarser stories, evoking hunted little glances of pleasure and a squeaky, guilty laughter.

I doubt if she had ever had such a friend. She had lived here all her life, but she had no intimates among the villagers. She had little to do with the bullying old lady who employed her as a needlewoman. Her only social occupations were to go to church regularly and to perform, in the evenings, errands of charity for the vicar. Nobody ever called on her. Everybody in the village smiled dutifully at her, uttered polite greetings, flicked their unfelt pity across her face and went their complacent ways. The vicar probably regarded her as a slight nuisance. The poor people whom she visited were stubbornly and remotely respectful. When she was at home she sat at her window, alone, reading or sewing. The only gaiety for her was in her visits to us, and then only when Ted was at hand. When he was away, I was the one she talked to, and although she used to smile up at me as eagerly as she did to Ted, I was unable to give her the response she craved. After a few minutes of painful conversation she would turn away without warning, clamber on to her bicycle and lurch off in a perilous panic.

One evening she had been hanging about me for a half-hour, the dumb fixity of her gaze worrying me to the point of resentment. Ted was away, and I assumed that she was waiting for his return. I told her that we expected him back at any moment, but we had reached a point at which neither of us could think of anything more to say, and she muttered good evening, ran to the door and mounted her bicycle. She was even clumsier than usual, standing on the pedals, her head lowered, the machine swerving across the road in a little spurt of speed each time she pressed a foot down. Between the tall hedges her movements were as blind and pathetic as those of a moth blundering about inside a lampshade.

A hundred yards from the billet door, the road turned sharply and climbed a small hill. As I stood watching the hunchbacked woman, a sound came to my ear. I turned and glimpsed our platoon truck swooping down the hill. It vanished in the dip behind the hedgerows. There was no time for a warning. The bicycle was moving in a wide slow swerve towards the corner as the truck flashed out from behind the hedge. A long, sustained screech of brakes, nerve-racking, the truck skidding broadside across the lane, the crash of its front wheels through the hedge, the clatter of the bicycle falling: and silence. The rear wheel of the bicycle spun slowly, purring. The woman lay face downward across the road. Ted climbed out of the truck's cab and walked towards her.

He had turned her over when I arrived, and was wiping blood and dust from her face. 'She's all right. Stunned her for a minute, that's all.'

'You sure? Careful how you move her.'

She opened her eyes and looked up at us wonderingly.

'I didn't hit her,' Ted said. 'She fell off as I went past.'

Men had come to the door of the billet. Others, who had been sunbathing in the field, were running towards us.

'You're all right, love,' Ted said to the woman. 'I'm a naughty boy, a'n' I?'

She nodded, smiled and closed her eyes again. He gathered her up in his arms and lifted her easily. 'I'll take her in to her place.'

I went with him. The front door was unlocked, and we entered the little parlour. There was a settee, and I walked towards it, but Ted went on through another door into the bedroom. I followed. He laid the woman on her bed and took her shoes off. He told me to get some water and a towel.

There was a washstand with a jug and basin on it. This, with the bed and the plain wooden wardrobe, was the only furniture. There was a mirror over the washstand, and on the wall near the door a coloured engraving of the Redeemer blessing the little children. I poured water and brought the basin across to the bed. Ted washed and wiped the woman's face and hands. She was unhurt except for abrasions on her forehead.

'It was my fault,' she muttered humbly. 'I wasn't looking where I was going.'

'I'll get the doctor,' I said. 'Best if he has a look at you.'

'Oh, no,' she cried, in a panic. 'I'm all right. I only fell off. It was my fault, I never look where I'm going. Really!'

'She's all right,' Ted said. 'She don't want no doctor.' He smiled down at her. 'It wasn't nobody's fault, duck. Don't you fret. Head ache?'

'Only a weeny bit.'

'Soon fix that. Where's your medicine chest?'

She told us. We put dressings on her forehead and gave her some aspirins. While Ted dabbed at the grazes I sat on the edge of the bed. Her hand moved across the coverlet and clutched mine. It was as cold as marble: shock.

'I'll fill a hot-water bottle,' I said. 'And I'll make you a nice cup of tea.'

I rose to go, but she would not release my hand. 'Stay here,' she cried. Her unnatural urgency, and the strength of her grip, made me wonder if the shock had sent her mind wandering.

I freed my hand. 'I'll be back in a minute. Ted'll stay here with you.'

When I came back she was under the blankets, her dress and stockings hanging over the bedside chair. I would never have dared to undress this poor little monster of modesty, but Ted must have done it as a matter of course, as if he were putting one of his own two children to bed. The door had been open while I was out of the room, and I had not heard any variation of protest or persuasion in the even murmur of their voices. She was shivering now, and we put the hot-water bottle at her feet. I sat by the bed and held the teacup to her lips. She sipped, and once more took my free hand in hers. Ted was speaking, but she looked at me all the time. I was unsettled. I felt that she was trying to say something which I could not understand. Then it came to me: perhaps she wanted me to go.

The shock had passed away and now, in reaction, her temperature was rising. Her forehead was flushed and moist, her hand had become feverishly hot. Why should she want me to go? Had Ted's kindness aroused in her some dumb, hopeless, horrible adoration? It could be nothing more than that. Hero-worship, I decided: a child's desire to be left alone with a favourite.

Before I could make any move to leave, Ted had risen from his place. 'I'm going to get the truck out of the hedge. You stay for a bit.'

I expected the woman to make some movement or utterance of disappointment, but she remained quiet and passive, still holding my hand.

He said to her, 'I'll put that bike of yours away. You shut your eyes and try to go to sleep. He'll stay with you.'

It was not my intention to spend an evening in this little room: there was not enough charity in me. I stood up, taking my hand away from the woman's, and ignoring the mournful, upward look she threw me, said to Ted, 'No, you stay. I've got to get back to the billet, anyway. I'll get one of the fellows to see about the truck.'

He did not pause in his stride as he crossed the room. I added, meanly, 'You heard me.' He stopped, and looked at me intently and dangerously. I knew that my objection meant nothing to him, but that he would not hurt the woman's feelings by quarrelling with me as to who should stay. He made a curt little gesture of dismissal to me with his head. Then he went back to the bedside. I left, feeling ashamed and annoyed.

I drove the truck, which was undamaged although its paintwork was marked, back to the billet, and sent one of the men to put the woman's bicycle away in its little shed.

The evening passed. We lay about in the field, dozed, talked, played cards. Ted did not come out of the house. The clouds heaped up in the west, the sunset glowing through them in many subtle colours. The fire died out of them, and they lay in purple masses, growing darker and darker. The sky between them was infused with shadow, and the shadow thickened into night. Ted had still not returned. Ribald jokes began to pass among the men. They recalled his calm accounts of many conquests. He had once told us a ludicrous and horrible tale about a love affair he claimed to have had with a pair of Siamese twins, and he had jeered happily at those of the men who had been simple enough to believe the story and squeamish enough to utter expressions of disgust. I told them that he was only staying to keep the woman company, but I was still too resentful against him to defend him with any persistence, and I fell silent, while the gossip and laughter flowed on around me. A light had been burning in the bungalow, showing through the blackout curtains like a faint phosphorescence. It was extinguished. We went to bed.

In the morning Ted's bed was still unoccupied. He appeared after breakfast and, without greeting any of us, went to work on his truck, washing the mud from the scratched wings and repainting them. The rest of us had a training parade, and we did not see him until lunchtime. He sat down at the long wooden table and ate his meal in silence. None of the crude jokes that were directed at him received an answer. At each remark Ted would glance at the speaker as if noticing an insect on the table, then go on with his eating.

In the evening he came back from a run to headquarters and gave out the mail, talking quite ordinarily with us all but seeming not to hear anything that was said to him about the hunchbacked woman.

Another day went by, and although the first wave of excited surmise had died down in the billet, the men still gave Ted no peace. What had originally been mere speculation was now accepted as fact, and Ted's contemptuous impassivity only stung the men to rail among themselves at him like rebuked children. They told each other that it was a bit rotten, what he had done, and that you wouldn't catch them doing a thing like that. From time to time I repeated my conviction that nothing had happened, but although it would have been natural for me to ask Ted what had taken place after I left, I was shy of mentioning the matter to him while the rest of the men were still assailing him with their questions and jibes. He, for his part, said nothing to me, and to anyone else who approached him he would only answer, 'Nasty little tyke, ain't you?' or, 'You'll die of curiosity one day if you don't look out,' or simply, 'Beat it, you annoy me.' More often, he would flash a brief, scornful glance at the speaker and go on with his work. For the most part, his bearing was one of placid unconcern, as if he were unaware that anything worthy of comment had taken place.

It was on the third morning after the accident, when I was left behind in the billet as orderly, that I had a chance to talk with Ted. The cook had brought us a bucket of thick, sweet tea, and we sprawled against the table, drinking.

I said, 'I wonder how she's feeling. I went over yesterday but she was out. Cookie says he saw her going off to work.'

'She's all right.'

'You seen her?'

'No.'

'How d'you know, then?'

'She went to work the morning after. I told her to. Best thing she could do.'

A pause.

'Here,' I said, 'what happened, that night?'

He looked at me with contempt. 'You an' all?'

'Well, I mean, I wondered. I told the chaps you were just sitting up with her.'

Another glance, as if wondering whether to take me seriously. 'Are you kidding?'

My face must have betrayed my feelings. He laughed brutally. 'The boy's disappointed in me. Look at him!'

I shrugged my shoulders. 'I just don't understand, that's all. Doing a thing like that.'

'A thing like that!' The sudden blaze of strength in his voice surprised me. 'Ah!' He sounded tired again. 'Away and leave me be.'

'I'm sorry. I didn't mean to be inquisitive.' I had finished my tea and I rose to leave.

He watched me for a few seconds, then he said, 'What would you say if I told you something?'

'Told me what?'

Again a few moments of silence while he studied me. 'You're a big boy now. Sit down.'

I obeyed.

'You're the one she's sweet on,' he said. 'She calls you "the shy one".'

I could not do anything but stare; and I was so stupefied by what he had said that I did not take in his next remark. Vaguely aware that he had spoken again, I said, 'What's that?'

He repeated, in a tone of weary bitterness, 'Did you reckon there was some that aren't entitled to it?'

I made a helpless grimace.

'It's the bane of life,' he said.

I cried, 'It's not!'

'You'll live to curse it.'

I was not prepared to cope at once with so new a view of life. I said, 'How did you find out? What happened with her, anyway?'

'When you walked out. She cried. She told me all about it. I reckon the shake-up must have loosened her tongue. She'd never have spoken otherwise. It all came up like spew. I don't reckon she knew what she was saying. I'm certain she couldn't have stopped herself. Well, she's never talked to a soul like that before, and I don't reckon she will again.'

'What happened then?'

It was his turn to grimace, in a kind of self-mockery. 'Once she'd spilled it all she was half-dead with shame. She couldn't look at me. I couldn't bear to look at her, for that matter. I couldn't walk out. There was nothing to say. Only one thing to do, and I did it.'

'Didn't she try to stop you?'

He scrutinised my face, as if still wondering whether I could be serious. 'You don't understand, do you?'

I shook my head.

'You will when you grow up.' A dry laugh. 'She had her arms round my neck. She nearly throttled me. Tell me,' he added, a tightening of irony in his voice, 'what would you have done?'

For the first time I was confronted squarely with the question that, years later, I still cannot answer: how—*how*—ought we to live? I answered desperately, 'I don't know.' He waited for me to say something else. I had nothing to add. I asked, 'What happened then?'

'Nothing.'

'Didn't you talk?'

'No.'

'Not all night?'

'No.'

'What, you just lay there, all night?'

'With her arms round me. And silent as the grave.'

'But she must have said something in the morning?'

'Such as what?'

I shrugged my shoulders. 'But when you left? Didn't she say anything? How did she look? Glad, or sorry, or what?'

'She kept the blanket over her face.'

'And didn't you say anything?'

'What was there to say? She wanted to be left alone. When I got to the door, I said, "You ought to go in to work today."'

'What did she say?'

'Nothing. Then I said, "Don't stay at home thinking. Go to work."'

'And then?'

'And then nothing. I went out. She went to work. What do you want, a happy ending?'

The White Domain

In six years of soldiering a lot of unexpected jobs crop up. Once I went to sea and learned the rules of navigation. Once I became a coalman, parading the streets of Tidworth with horse and cart and a magnificent hat that had a long leather flap hanging down at the back. I was a docker for a month and a nursemaid for two days; and once I was top man in a human pyramid.

What I am going to write about now is the period, in nineteen forty-two when I had a taste of what it is like to be a miner.

An underground headquarters was to be built. The job involved boring a network of tunnels into a cliff face, eighty feet down from the top. As several million soldiers were at that time waiting in Britain for the Second Front to open, it was not difficult for the authorities to bring together a couple of hundred former miners to do the skilled work and another few hundred unskilled men, of whom I was one, to work as labourers.

For six months I lived in a little community of miners. They came from every coalfield in the country, and there were innumerable variations of accent, personality and behaviour among them, but they all seemed to be united by some secret understanding. The outsider felt as if some vibration of sympathy, on a wavelength unknown to him, was passing among them.

They were like no other soldiers I ever met. They got on well with their officers, who were quiet and efficient men accustomed to managing big construction jobs. There was a tacit agreement between officers and men that speed and discipline were needed. But the respect, on the miners' part, always seemed conditional. They carried themselves like men who were observing their side of a coalfield agreement rather than like soldiers under the shadow of the King's Regulations. They had their own way of standing to attention, not slackly but—so to speak—with tolerance.

Most of them were tall and well built, and in the open air they had a freedom and boldness in their gait that suggested Melville's Handsome Sailor rather than the stunted miner, the Black Dwarf of fiction. Everything about them contributed to this nautical appearance. All of them, whether they were ugly or fair, had a rare firmness of countenance, an inherited character of complete but unstrained inner control shining out of their faces. The same discipline controlled their voices, so that however violently they raised them, there was never that ugly rowdiness that rings in the voices of other young workmen.

They were deadly with women—not loutish and loud and fundamentally uncertain, like most of us others, but swift, intense and confident. They had their own way of getting drunk, blackly and inwardly. Instead of fuddling them, drink concentrated their faculties, endowing them in appearance with the silent menace of the leopard about to leap. They seldom fought, but when they did they were murderous.

I never met among them any of the dark philosophers or other learned characters who are supposed to abound in mining communities. The only books I ever saw among them were a racing form book and a pornographic masterpiece. The only interest common to them all was gambling, which they practised in a spirit of calm and cheerful madness. Nevertheless they were good to listen to. They excelled in a light and deadly banter. Pride rang in their speech. They could express themselves fully, sparely and vigorously in peasant-born idioms—Scottish, Northumbrian, Midlands or Welsh—that made the fragmentary, childish speech of the urban under-educated among us sound like ape-talk. Few of them were conscious of any interest in politics, but the exclusiveness of their class, like the Catholicism of medieval man, was a lens through which they saw all human affairs. To them, Churchill was a cunning old dog whom you had to admire, Stalin was 'Old Dirt-box' (a name whose irreverent but friendly implications no Communist could ever understand), and Attlee was 'that wee mannie'.

They kept to themselves. Whenever any group of them assembled to do a job, there was never any need for previous discussion, even if they were all strangers to each other. No one took charge, and they did not shout advice to each other, but they all took their places and moved as harmoniously through their task as a *corps de ballet*.

This is how we worked. Some of the miners drove a pilot tunnel, breaking up the chalk with pneumatic picks, which they called 'windy picks'. Others followed, enlarging the tunnel to its final diameter and shoring it with girders and wooden slats. We labourers followed, laying a narrow-gauge railway, running wheeled tubs along the line (each 'tub' consisted of an iron trolley, with flanged steel wheels, on which the tub rested within a frame), shovelling into these tubs the chalk the miners excavated, and carting it away.

The miners had cut the tunnel floor so that the last few hundred yards sloped down to the exit; and at the cliff face the emptied chalk had formed a tip, on to whose levelled surface we ran the tubs.

Try, then, to imagine the scene. In a bay deep underground, two miners are drilling into the chalk. They are naked to the waist, covered with a paste of chalk and sweat, and they work like white demons. There are four of us crouching in the tiny cave, the two miners and two labourers, and our ears are deafened by the hammering din of the picks and the crash of falling chalk. There is a pale, sickening light, reflecting on the rugged white surfaces, from an electric bulb slung in a wire shield from a girder behind us. The air, already used to drive the picks, smells burned and rubbery from the pump, and is hung with stifling chalk-dust. The miners, without mercy for their two slaves, drive on into the chalk; and we, killing ourselves to match their pace, shovel chalk into the tub behind us, then put our shoulders to the tub and push it away down the line.

For a long time—to us it seems to have no end—we push the full weight of the tub, lying almost full-length behind it. Our tub winds and clatters through the long main tunnel, while from bay after bay to right and left comes the white glare of electric light upon the chalk, and the roar of picks, a noise that stops the ears. At each junction there is a turntable, usually out of alignment, which resists the wheels of the tub and threatens to spill it.

Then we reach the top of the last slope. Ahead, like a target, can be seen the circle of daylight or of cool blue night—for we work in an endless round of eight-hour shifts—and we imagine that we can already taste the sweet air. One man goes back to start filling the next tub. The other leaps on to the back of the tub as it starts down the slope of its own volition. With a ton of chalk and a man aboard, the tub gathers speed until it is rumbling down to the exit too fast to be stopped. At last, clattering like an express train, it shoots out into the fresh air. The man riding on the back breathes deeply and gratefully, and as the tub slows down, he drops off and trots behind. Crude buffers bring the tub to a stop. The tub is built in its frame to swivel over sideways, and the man empties it, watching the boulders of chalk go bounding away down the steep tip-face. Then he squats on the edge of the trolley and waits. Soon his mate will arrive aboard another tub, and the two of them will combine to push the two empty tubs back into the tunnel by another entrance.

For me, as for all the unskilled men, this work was very hard at first. The miners were not hostile. They taught us our jobs and looked to our safety. But they excluded us from their fellowship, and they did not conceal their contempt for our awkwardness and our ill-repressed fear. Sometimes they played practical jokes on us, scaring us with their familiar perils. Soon after my arrival on the job, one of them invited me to try my hand with the 'windy pick'. It seemed easy enough. I took up the pick and found that it was several times heavier than it looked. I put the point against the chalk, leaned on it and pressed with the flat of my hand on the plate inside the spade grip that released the compressed air. Instead of the point biting into the chalk it merely tapped at it, while on the other end of the pick I vibrated like a fever-stricken jelly. When the miners had had their laugh, they showed me how to place my feet, how to brace my body, how to hold the pick locked firm against the chalk-face. Then they invited me to try again. One thing they had not shown me—where to place the point, an art on which lives could depend and which each of them had spent his whole working lifetime acquiring. I pressed the grip and this time the pick stabbed into the chalk; but—as the miners, moving quietly out of the bay, had foreseen—I brought down what felt like a couple of hundredweight of the roof upon my head. They hauled me out and dusted me down with great punishing swipes, and one of them said, 'It's all right, feller, we knew it wouldn't kill you.'

I got used to this kind of thing, and in time, when I had learned enough about the job, took pleasure in it, particularly when I was present at the initiation of further newcomers. Still, it was no parlour game. The work, difficult and dangerous enough in normal times, was being carried out at higher speed than in civilian life, and without the accustomed safety and health precautions. The miners seemed to enjoy it, tearing into the job like assault troops. We others had to get acclimatised as best we could.

I worked for a Scottish miner named Kinney. He was a silent, solitary man who had no more than an occasional grunt for his own friends and no time to talk to me. The first few weeks I suffered from fainting fits. Kinney watched but said nothing. One day a Tyneside miner said to me, 'You're sweat'n' too much, kidda. Eat more salt.' I got some salt pills from the sick bay to replace the excessive loss, and was cured. I said to Kinney, 'Didn't you know about the salt?' He grinned, and answered, 'Ah'm not y'r mammy, laddie.'

At first, when we worked together, he would leave me far behind. I would shovel in weary desperation while the heaps of chalk grew in front of me. Then I began to catch up with him. I had no trouble now, except with the pockets of foul air we ran into, in which he thrived, but which made me vomit and, once or twice, collapse. There was a little interchange between us which became a routine. From time to time during the shift he would stop hewing and look back to see where I was. I, sweating at his heels, would say, '—you, mate, I'm still here,' and he, with a wicked little grin, would turn back to his work. That—although it would be wrong to say that we disliked each other—summed up the relationship between us.

One night we were working at especially high pressure. We had filled one tub, and my mate had taken it away to the tip. Slaving on my own (the shovel had the biggest blade I have ever seen; to me it looked as big as a tea-tray, and when it was laden I could hardly lift it) I had filled two more tubs.

Kinney looked back and remarked that we were in danger of getting a traffic jam.

I said that I would take a tub out if he would give me a push down the tunnel with it. I might have tried to do it myself, but we were working in bad air and I felt sick and sluggish.

He replied that it would be best to push both the tubs out to the last gradient. Then I could ride out on the first tub, and he would follow on the other. He wanted a blow, anyway.

We pushed the two tubs up to the head of the exit slope. As we lay straining behind them, he spoke to me, but I could not hear what he was saying. The blood was going to my lowered head. The uproar in the tunnel seemed to be growing worse than ever, full of booming echoes, the fumes more sickening. I wondered if I would faint or vomit before I could get rid of the foul air in my lungs, and was frightened of the last thundering rush ahead of me.

Kinney was waiting for me to take the first tub away. There was no time to hesitate. We both pushed, the tub started away, I jumped on the back and clung, crouching. Faster than regret, I was borne away.

The tub was rolling, gathering speed under the weight of its load. Hanging at the back, with my backside down near the ground and my arms extended over my head as I clung to the crossbar above me, I was hit by quick blows of nausea. I was in no condition to let loose the screeching war-whoops with which we usually advertised our coming to those on the tip.

Faster and faster, the tub rattled and swayed as it rode the curving rails towards the last bend. Then, unexpectedly, a last waft of foul air, a beastly sewer smell, a stifling of my breath as if a sponge pad were being pressed to my face. I fainted.

What happened after that I learned from other people. I fell across the rails. I must have knocked my head, for I remained unconscious, and there was a lump afterwards. The tub, unmanned, shot away and ran out on to the tip.

Almost immediately the next tub, with Kinney riding on the back of it, came down the slope.

He saw me. He was travelling fast. There were only a few yards to go. I cannot imagine that he had more than a second in which to make up his mind.

In this second he had to decide among the following courses.

He could continue to cling to the tub and be caught in the spill when the heavy flanged wheels smashed through me.

He could drop off the back of the tub, saving himself from injury while the tub ran on to hit me.

Or—this was what he did. He kept his hold on the frame and flung his weight to the right. The wrench lifted the front wheels slightly off the rails and to the left. The tub left the rails and crashed at full speed into the soft chalk wall on the left-hand side of the tunnel, a couple of yards short of where I was lying.

Kinney dropped clear as he felt the tub leap off the line, but he was flung backwards to the ground by the speed. The impact of the tub against the wall brought down a fall of roof, a mass of chalk which buried the tub. Some of the rubble fell upon us, but not enough to do more than add to the number of our bruises.

That was all. Silence. Drifting chalk-dust. The yellow electric glare. Shouts and the clatter of boots as men who had heard the crash came running.

Both of us soon recovered. Within twenty minutes we were sitting side by side on the tip, enjoying the cool night air.

Kinney squatted next to me, silent and still, as self-absorbed as a cat in front of the fire. I, too, remained quiet, thinking about the incident. I decided not to thank him. His attitude seemed to warn me against it.

There was, to him, no reason for thanks. He had acted, as he would have expected any of his comrades to act, instinctively. Since the act sprang from the normal fabric of his life, he could not have perceived any cause in it for comment.

It sprang from the oneness of his kind. Between one man and another there was complete reliance and understanding. They would work together in a bay where the roof threatened to fall in. Without exchanging a word, they would go on working to within a few seconds of the fall. Then, a glance from one to another sufficing, they would move out just in time.

For centuries their kind had been developing these instincts and skills, and the ability to know what was in each other's minds. They came of a stock in whose blood ran the knowledge that, tombed in their mile-deep mineshafts, the lives of all of them depended on entire and instantaneous accord. Each man accepted mutual dependence as an inheritance, the readiness to act without thought for others, the confidence that the others would act in the same way.

This was the true difference between them and those others of us who live in the world like unintegrated atoms.

In Kinney's place I might have done as he did. I hope so, and I hope that I would have been able to think quickly enough.

But my first instinct, the first need that would have rung its signals in me, with only that second in which to overcome it, would have been to save myself.

Kinney's first instinct, when he saw me lying across the rails, was to save the other man. It was not a thought which came to him in that second. It was in his father's seed from which he grew.

If I did not thank him, then, it was not out of ingratitude, but because I wanted to make full recognition of the man himself, of what he was.

He rose to his feet and said sternly, 'Are ye fit to finish the shift?'

We got back during the half-time break. The men were resting, some reading papers, some eating sandwiches. Four of the miners were squatting round a slab of chalk, playing cards, and others were standing around them.

They gave us quick, hard glances of welcome, but no smiles or spoken greetings. Kinney joined the intent, silent circle round the card-players.

Their naked backs were powdered grey and runnelled with sweat. They wore soiled denim trousers tied at the ankles, and big boots thick with chalk. But, clustered in the electric glare, amid the caverns of their white domain, with their fierce youthful faces and relaxed arrogance of bearing, they looked like some Renaissance painting of a group of young princes, plotting to hasten their inheritance.

Old Beethoven

L istening to a Beethoven piano concerto, I remembered Tom Meredith.
Music sets my dreams free; it is nearly always Beethoven. A storm of harmony subsides, leaving a lucent groundswell of melody. Into the lakelike calm the piano enters with little cascades of music, ripples of high pure notes that fall as softly as tears into the wider flow. The waves run again, surge smoothly, mount and break once more in vast proclamatory chords. All the weight of human passion is crashing down upon the listener, thundering about him. Consciousness is drowned; blind eddies of agitation reach down into the depths; and, all unbidden, memories are drawn up to the mind's surface.

On this evening, as I listened to the fourth piano concerto, it was the forgotten face of Tom Meredith that rose to haunt me.

In nineteen forty-three when he was twenty and I was five years older, our unit was waiting to go overseas. Our past training and the equipment we had received warned us that we were going to take part in an assault from the sea—somewhere. I cannot remember whether we were afraid. It was unlikely, for we were young, fit and too confident. Certainly, however, we were afflicted by a kind of stage fright, an iciness and a rending impatience at the core of our high spirits; and the need to hold this down increased our determination to have a good time in the few days before we left.

At the beginning of the last week three of us, Tom, myself and an ex-bookmaker's runner from Liverpool named O'Toole, drew all our back pay and set out to spend it in town.

On Monday night we went the round of the pubs and lurched back to barracks spewing and singing discordantly.

On Tuesday night we went to the music hall. After the show we went round to the back door and persuaded three of the girls to come to supper with us. We were disappointed to find that, off the stage, they were just three pallid, tired and very cautious working-girls, but we were proud to have talked them into coming with us and we were quite satisfied to be dismissed with a few prim good-night kisses.

On Wednesday night we went, for the first time in any of our lives, to a good restaurant, and ate a black-market dinner. We had roast duckling and a bottle of wine. After a rest we had omelets and mushrooms, strawberries and cream and more wine. Then, while Tom and I were drinking little cups of black coffee, O'Toole, who liked to show off, had a lobster salad.

On Thursday night there was a gigantic party in the barracks, which ended up amid a good deal of wrecked furniture.

On Friday—

On Friday the three of us had very little money left and no idea how to pass the evening. We lounged about the town, thinking rather miserably that we ought to find something better than this to do on our last free night in England. We could not afford another night's drinking. We had seen all the films. We were still arguing what to do, vaguely and fruitlessly, when we came to the Civic Hall.

O'Toole said, 'Ah, bloody concert. Come on, there's nothing doing here.'

Tom and I hung about, looking at the people going in. Tom pointed at a poster. 'Chap playing the piano. I like to hear a chap that's good on the piano. Or the fiddle.'

I said, 'He's one of the best there is.'

'It's only half a dollar,' Tom said. 'We can always come out if we don't like it.'

O'Toole said, 'Bloody ideas you get sometimes!' But when we went in, he followed us.

We stayed to the end of the concert. We sat back in the gallery, arms folded, and frowned down upon the orchestra, not clapping when others clapped, making no comment in the intervals and pushing our way out at the end while the conductor was still bowing.

It was a lovely May night. The streets were full of moonlight. Each of us waited for the others to say something, but none of us spoke. We swung along, our steel-shod boots crashing loud on the deserted pavements. O'Toole said that there was time for a drink before the pubs closed. Tom said, 'Ah,—you and your drinks!' O'Toole stared at him, but kept loyally in step, and did not ask where we going even when, instead of returning to the barracks, we strode clear across town, over the Common and back through the silent outskirts. At midnight we walked into the billet.

O'Toole looked as if he were still waiting for one of us to say something, but he got nothing except 'Good night', and went off to his room looking puzzled.

A few days later we were at sea. For the first few days, in the North Atlantic, the ship was wrapped in mist. All we knew of the rest of the convoy was the sound of sirens. There was no feeling of movement except for the vibration of the decks and the beat of the ship's engines. We still did not know where we were going. It might have been unnerving if we had talked or even thought about this uncanny journey, about the hazards that might strike at us through the mists, or about what must lie at the end of it; but we did not.

We performed wearisome fatigues, attended boat drills, played housy-housy for hours at a time, queued interminably for cups of tea, read and lounged about the decks talking of trivialities. One morning Tom and I were taking a turn on deck. O'Toole was down below tidying the hammock lockers. Tom said, 'That was a week, wasn't it, before we went away?'

'I'll say!'

'Them tarts!'

'Smashing!'

'I could do with one of them right now, couldn't you?'

'Just right for this weather.'

'Just right for any weather.' A pause. 'Here, how do you say that name again? Chap wrote that music?'

'What music?'

'Up the Town Hall that night.'

'Beethoven.'

'Beethoven.' He pronounced the word carefully. 'Long time ago, wasn't he?'

'I reckon so.'

'When?'

'About Napoleon's time.'

'When was that about?'

'About a hundred and fifty years ago.'

'And they still play his pieces?'

'Yes.'

He made a sucking, wondering sound. 'Jus' shows you, eh?' I left him to his thoughts. A few moments later he said, 'About time we got in the tea queue, isn't it? Or we won't get served.'

The days passed; engines thumping; rough weather; the other ships in sight once more, dotted over the wide grey circle of sea; destroyers burying themselves in white masses of water and shaking themselves free; an aircraft alarm, din of guns and the empty sky stained with smoke; card games, concerts, rumours, rumours, rumours. Time become a dream. Into southern waters; sunlight sparkling on a blue sea; the men wearing shorts and bush shirts; a strange, dizzy, holiday feeling; rifles to be cleaned; physical training; the end of the dream approaching.

We came up on deck one day after a good lunch, all three of us. We leaned at the rails, watching the porpoises leap, shed dazzling drops of spray and thump back into the sea. Tom said, 'That was a treat. Tripe and onions for dinner. Not often you get that.'

'It's lucky half the chaps was sick,' O'Toole said. 'I ate till I bust and there was still some left in the tin. It breaks your heart to leave it.'

'I'm not seasick,' Tom said.

'I'm not seasick neither,' O'Toole said. 'What about you?'

'Seasick?' I said. 'Me? You're daft.'

'Who's daft?'

'The pair of you.'

'Well,' Tom said. 'I like that! Here, I was thinking. This feller—'

I said, 'What feller?'

'Old Beethoven.' He uttered the name quite unexpectedly. We had not mentioned it since that morning together on deck; and now he spoke as if of an old friend.

O'Toole asked, 'Who's he?'

Tom answered, 'Chap wrote that music.'

'What music?'

'Up the Town Hall that night, daft!'

'Ha! That night! Bloody night that was!' He glared at Tom. 'Your bloody clever idea, that was!'

'I reckon it was.'

'Reckon it was what?'

'A bloody good idea. Here, look—' Tom turned to me. 'Old Beethoven, that tune of his they played, that wasn't one tune we heard there, was it? It was about twenty. I was trying to remember it, and first I remembered one tune—well, you know, a bit of it—and then I remembered another. And then I forgot that one and I thought of another one altogether. Here, well I reckon there was about twenty tunes in that piece, at least, and they all went in together, and that sort of made the one big tune.' He waited anxiously for my opinion.

'I reckon that's the idea of it,' I said. 'That's why composers like him are famous. It's not just one tune they write. It's a whole, sort of, pattern of music, and they weave it all together. There's anything from fifty instruments upwards in those orchestras, and he writes a separate part for each of them. Only they all harmonise.'

Tom asked, 'Do you reckon he thinks of them one at a time or all together?'

'Well, I don't know really.'

'Still,' he said, 'it's clever. He must think of them all at once or he wouldn't—' He broke off, and then exclaimed in a tone of deep awe, 'All that in one man's head!'

'You know what I think?' O'Toole said.

'What, daft?'

'I think we're going to Russia. Through the Dardanelles. Get in behind the Jerries there and finish them off.'

An old argument started again.

A few days later the argument was settled. We swarmed out of the ship's sally ports into a white glare of sunshine, crammed into one of the little landing-craft that wallowed on the slow, sickening swell, crouched helmeted and heavily burdened for hours on a hot steel deck amid the reek of oil and at last landed, tired, ill and sweating, on a beach in Sicily.

A new world, as unreal as the world of the sea; a succession of broken dreams, good dreams and bad dreams; on the move all the time yet not feeling that we were going anywhere; unaware of the things we were doing, only feeling that things were being done to us; blinding sunlight, bright colours, mosquitoes, thirst, muffling, parching white dust; days that were quiet and drowsy and nights that were fearsomely alive, riven by the noise, the racking fear and the firework flashes of war.

Three weeks later the advance along the coast had ended and the three of us were in a slit trench looking out across a broad bare plain. Across the plain, invisible but watching to strike down any man who tried to move forward, were the enemy.

We had a bad time there. The sun beat down upon us and sucked the strength out of us. Our uniforms clung to us uncomfortably, sodden black with sweat. We could not wash to keep cool or drink enough to keep thirst at bay, for water was scarce. The wells stank, for the Germans had polluted them with dead animals, and the water from them tasted evilly of chlorine. The sweet stench of unburied dead, men and beasts, hung upon the air. The white dust drifted and tormented. There were mosquitoes and malaria. The Germans had their snipers everywhere, and it was dangerous to show ourselves above ground by daylight. We huddled, ill and miserable, in our burning little holes in the ground.

The time had to be passed somehow. We talked.

I sat at one end of the trench, my knees up, reading a magazine. Tom was in the middle, staring at the brown wall as if he could see through a mile or two of solid earth into the pits where other men sat facing us. O'Toole was huddled at the other end with his eyes shut, his head lolling on one side, breathing heavily. He had dysentery. He was too weak by now to crawl to a latrine when his spasms came; in any case, with the snipers active, it was hardly worth the risk. He kept a biscuit tin by him, and from time to time one of us would empty it for him. His trousers were soaked with blood and slime. The tin made the close little pocket of overheated air in the trench smell horrible, and it attracted the flies in beastly black swarms, so that whenever we tried to eat we had to brush them off every scrap of food.

Tom said, 'How long we been here?'

I closed my magazine. 'I don't know. About three weeks.'

'What? In this place?'

'I thought you meant in Sicily.'

'Oh,' he said wearily. 'Sicily!' He closed his eyes and leaned his head back against the wall of the trench, swearing softly at Sicily.

'It's Friday. We dug in here Tuesday night.'

We lit cigarettes and blew smoke up at the parapet. Tom asked O'Toole if he wanted a smoke. O'Toole shook his head feebly without opening his eyes and fumbled for his water-bottle. Tom helped him to drink and put the water-bottle away.

In the distance we heard the faint crack of a sniper's rifle. We listened. Silence. Tom said, 'Give us one of your sweets. For him.'

We had a ration of boiled sweets. They were the only food that O'Toole could keep in his mouth without vomiting, and the sugar in them kept his strength up. I passed my pack to Tom. He rummaged, and pushed a sweet between O'Toole's lips. 'What the *bloody* hell are we doing here?' he burst out. 'Call this a war?'

'It's a war all right. Stick your head over the top and find out.'

'It makes you wonder. How did we *get* here? Listen, I'll tell you what. I can't remember *coming* here!'

'I can't remember ever being anywhere else.'

'I—' He had sat up, straining to think. He relaxed again. 'Phew! It's too bloody hot to remember anything.'

We both went off into a waking doze; for how long, I cannot remember. It may have been an hour or two. I opened my magazine again, but my gaze rested on the words without taking them in.

It was the sound of another shot that roused us; the distant crack and the faint glassy echoing of shouts in the hot stillness of the day. Men were calling for stretcher-bearers.

Tom said, 'I suppose he was one of them.'

'Who?'

'Old Beethoven. He was a Jerry, wasn't he?'

'Yes.' I was too dull and heat-struck to feel any surprise at the casual introduction of the name after all these weeks.

'That's a bloody laugh, eh?' He spoke without interest, not looking at me but continuing to gaze vacantly at the wall of earth in front of him.

'There's good and bad everywhere.'

'That's not what they tell you.'

I said, 'He was deaf.'

'What's that got to do with it?

'Nothing. I just thought.'

He looked at me, and traces of life came back into his face. 'How could he be, anyway?'

'Why not?'

'A deaf musician? You got the bloody sunstroke or something.'

'It was all in his head. He wrote some of his greatest music, and he conducted the orchestra that played it, but he couldn't hear them. That's another reason why they call him a genius.'

'Genius!' Tom's voice was awake now, awake with pain. 'Bloody torture I call it! Think of writing all that *lovely* bloody music and not being able to hear it. Here, if that was me, my bloody head would burst. All that music thundering away inside. Burst your head, it would.' Wonder lent animation to his eyes, and strength to his voice. 'I tell you what, though, that feller was a Man. A real, bloody Man, eh?' It took him a few seconds to recover from the articulation of this thought. Then he said, 'Of course, we only heard one of his pieces, didn't we?'

'Well, one and a couple of smaller bits.'

'I should like to hear the rest of them. That's what I'm goin' to do one day. Hear all the bloody lot of them, I will. Here—' he looked at me, and an anguish of puzzlement flitted across his face. 'It's a funny thing I never heard of him before. I mean, I'm twenty! Years of my life behind me. How come I never heard of a chap like that, all those years?'

I shrugged my shoulders. 'Happens.'

'How did you know all this about him?'

'A book.'

'Where'd you get it?

'Up the library.'

'Library, eh? That's another lark I've never tried.'

'Sounds as if you'll have a busy time when you get back.'

'Ha! I will! I'll— You're right there, I will an' all. What else?'

'About him? Well, he was a very independent chap. He was a bit of a rebel. He was all for freedom, and all that kind of thing. One day, some chap introduced himself, he said, "I'm So-and-so von So-and-so, Landowner." And old Beethoven bowed back, and he said, "And I'm Ludwig van Beethoven, Brain-owner."'

'Ha! There's the kiddie! *He* would, eh? It's gone quiet, hasn't it?' It was ten minutes since we had heard any sound of war.

'I tell you what,' he resumed. 'You were right, what you said. About having a busy time when I get back. When I get back, do you know what I want to do?' His whole body came alive, and before I could restrain him he straightened up, all upright and shining with youth, looking out over the parapet as if beyond the dismal plain was appearing all the bright beauty of the world that he had never seen. 'When I get back I want to—'

Those were his last words.

The Pillbox

One night during the Sicilian campaign a party of commandos, accompanied by a pioneer detachment, went ashore on a lonely stretch of coast to prepare the way for a larger-scale landing.

It was almost dawn, and the men climbed through a pine wood until they had reached the low ridge which dominated the beaches. They moved along the ridge to clear it of any defenders, but they found only a few forlorn groups of Italian soldiers whom they rounded up silently and without any difficulty.

The men, who had been spilled ashore full of the tension and hot vigour that long training and the lack of action had bottled up in them, grew cold and bored as they trudged in silent files along the bare slopes. The two officers at their head commiserated with each other upon the lack of excitement.

The sky grew lighter. By now the main body of landing-craft would be starting out from the troopships. There was no bombardment, for no considerable opposition was expected. The landing of the advance party had only been a precaution to ensure that no small groups of Italians who might happen to be hereabouts could establish themselves on the ridge to fire down on the beaches.

They came to a dip in the ridge and halted. Below them, in the saddle of ground, they saw a concrete pillbox sunk into the seaward crest of the ridge so that it commanded the beach. A man was just vanishing into the pillbox, and they saw the steel door close.

The commando officer said to his colleague, 'All right, old man. I think we can manage this one without your chaps.'

'I beg your pardon,' the pioneer replied. 'It looks to me like a job for us.' The two young men continued to wrangle over the problem.

'I'll tell you what we'll do,' the commando said, and produced a coin. They tossed, and the pioneer won. 'Ours, I think,' he announced happily, and called his men forward while the commandos retired.

The pioneer officer had just begun to dispose his men when a white flag appeared outside the pillbox and a group of Italian soldiers emerged behind it.

'Oh, damn!' The officer stood with his hands on his hips, a picture of disappointment. 'The windy rotten bastards! All that lovely training, and all this lovely gelignite, and look what they've gone and done to us!'

The commando officer, who was sitting on the slope above him with his assault rations on his knees as if he were preparing for a picnic, said, 'Tickle 'em up with the Bren, old boy, and see what happens. We don't have to worry any more about making a noise.'

The pioneer officer took a light machinegun from one of his men and fired a couple of bursts from the hip. The Italians hesitated in bewilderment. The firing continued, and they scrambled back into the shelter of the pillbox. They continued to wave their white flag desperately. A couple more bursts sprayed the entrance, and they were forced to slam the steel door to protect themselves.

'There!' the commando said. 'Always listen to uncle. You can go ahead now, they're resisting.'

The Bren continued to fire at the slits in the pillbox. The white flag, which was protruding and wagging frantically, was withdrawn. A few moments later the inmates, blindly trying to at least keep these implacable attackers at bay, fired a few harmless shots.

'Now, my old sport,' the pioneer officer said, 'we'll give you a little demonstration in the use of high explosives, demolition. If you'll kindly pay attention.'

He and his men worked their way around the pillbox. While the commandos sat on the hillside brewing up tea, the pioneers laid their charges. They demolished the pillbox and its crew most efficiently, and made their way up the hill to join the commandos at breakfast.

A friend of mine, a mild and peaceable young man, took part in this episode and told it to me as a joke. Sometimes, when I hear myself making free with expressions like 'the humanist outlook' and 'the sanctity of life', I remember that for a couple of years after the event, I, too, continued to tell it to other people as a funny story.

The Music Box

We had entered the town the night before, from the landward side, and now, before noon, we were scrambling down the cobbled streets towards the harbour.

From the hills on which we had stood the previous day the little Sicilian port had looked like a picture-postcard town, gleaming white and tantalising. Now the beauty had vanished like a mirage. Shelling and air bombardment had left gaping houses, cobblestones heaved up as if by an earthquake, heaps of stinking refuse in the gutters, great mounds of rubble and splintered timber disfiguring the squares.

Behind us there were still streets ablaze. Smoke and dust befouled the air. But it was quiet at last in the town. There was no more cracking of snipers' rifles or disjointed quarrel of machineguns; only the crackle of flames, the occasional roar of an exploding mine, and the slither and crunch of our boots as we picked our way through the debris.

We saw few people. Most of the inhabitants had fled. Some were still cowering in their cellars. Only a few very old men and women stood in the gutters and watched us uncomprehendingly. One old woman, with a dark wrinkled face and wispy white hair, clasped her hands in an attitude of prayer and, opening her toothless mouth, pointed into it to show us she was hungry. She did not speak, but whimpered like an animal.

We halted for a moment and several of the men gave biscuits to her, although our rations were almost gone. When we marched away, the old woman was sitting on a doorstep gnawing painfully at a biscuit with her pallid gums.

The sun was right up in the sky now. We were plastered with sweat and white dust, hungry and exhausted. I led the section into a deserted street and gave them permission to fall out. Before they broke ranks I repeated to them the orders we had received: to keep in the shade, not to wander off, not to enter the houses, which were full of booby-traps, and not to loot.

We prowled about, peering in through the windows of houses. The outsides of Italian buildings were always a hundred per cent Fascist. There were big slogans, boldly painted.

'Believe, Obey, Fight.'

'To Have Many Enemies Is To Have Much Honour.'

'Die Valorously For The Fascist Empire.'

But inside these houses there was no Fascism. Each front door opened straight into a living-room, and they were all the same: a big double bed, religious pictures on the walls, old-fashioned photographs of wedding groups and black-bordered portraits of dead parents, and everywhere, spilled on every floor, heaps of letters. It always used to seem to me in the war, in country after country, that every retreating soldier, every fleeing civilian, must have been the possessor of a hoard of letters. Scattered in despair they left a trail of broken stories across Europe.

I left the section and went down the street to fill water-bottles. Before I left them I said, 'Remember, keep out of those bloody houses. I'm fed up with scraping silly bastards off walls.'

When I returned the street was deserted. I put the dripping water-bottles down on a wall and went to look for the section.

A couple of blocks up the street there were some shops—the same kind of humble little shops that can be seen in the back streets of English towns—a tobacconist's, a grocer's, a dressmaker's. The window frames had been jerked awry by blast, with jagged teeth of glass still showing round the edges.

I found some of the section in an old-clothes shop. Some of them were cramming socks into their packs. One man was tearing up a shirt to use as cleaning-rags. Another was trying on a broad-brimmed trilby hat and another stood in front of a cracked mirror admiring himself in a straw boater. They followed me out of the shop, and we went to look for the others.

The rest of the section were next door, in a toyshop. It was not the kind of toyshop our children are used to, full of glamorous dolls, modern aircraft and mechanical wonders of every kind. It was the kind of place that belonged in a story book, with a little old man behind the counter and Pinocchio pressing his nose against the window-pane: a tiny, dusty den with only a few simple toys of wood and tin and coloured paper on its shelves.

A couple of the men had found a packet of coloured streamers and were flinging them at each other, the flimsy coils of pink and yellow and blue writhing through the gloom of the shop and settling on our heads and shoulders. Another was delightedly winding up a clockwork toy he had found, a little acrobat on a horizontal bar. The acrobat wore a cricket cap, a striped jersey and tights. There was a fierce black moustache painted across his face. When he was wound up he sprang stiffly over and over the bar until the spring ran down. My lance-corporal was blowing in vain through the mouthpiece of a broken cardboard trumpet and his friend, a Liverpool slaughterhouse worker, was tapping with his fingers on a tiny drum.

But the main attraction was a music box. It worked with a weight, and it seemed to play for ever, tinkling over and over again the same childish, silly little tune. The notes were clear, soft and fragile, like fine glass or a tiny dulcimer. One by one we came until we were all gathered round it, squatting silently, listening. I felt that the faint music was somehow hurting me, and looking at the other men, the nine villainous and filthy men in their soiled, sweat-sodden uniforms, leaning on their rifles and listening with sombre fascination, I knew that it was working upon them too. I had felt like this once before, when we had been passing a school at the end of an exhausting march, and the shrill voices of children had come to us, faintly.

The music box was still playing on the floor when we left the shop. We trudged away in silence. A half-hour later, when we were out of the town and moving along a dusty white road into the country, I could still hear in imagination the faint sweet tinkling, and I did not want anyone to talk to me.

For weeks after, when we were bivouacked in scented lemon groves, or huddled in slit trenches under the hammering heat, or squatting beneath trees groaning with dysentery, or lying in the darkness while the earth trembled with bombardment: while the misery and degradation of war ate more and more deeply into us, one or another of us would whistle to himself a vague and half-remembered fragment of music. It was the tune, childish and heart-breaking, that the music box had played.

The Dead Cart

We had just passed through a Sicilian village when the company's truck stopped. There were signs of a conference at the front of the convoy; then the sergeant-major called for me, and I got down from the truck with my ten men.

We were outside a long, low stone building, its walls blank except for a couple of barred windows, its massive iron-studded doors like those of a prison, its steep roof of curly red tiles overhanging the wall by several inches.

The officer, who was already kicking at the starter of his motor-cycle, told me to put a guard on the building and not to let anyone else in. He promised to send a relief as soon as possible.

The convoy moved off. My men were peering in at the door, and one of them asked, in a timid, boyish voice that I ought to have suspected, 'Corporal, can we go inside out of the sun?'

There was no other place nearby where they could shelter in the shade. I said, 'OK.' The last truck had vanished along the winding white road, and we were alone, in the sunlight and the silence.

I entered the building. With the dazzle of daylight behind me, I stood at the head of a stone staircase that ran steeply down against the front wall, with no rail on its outer side. Out of the darkness, which gradually thinned into a clear gloom as my eyes grew used to it, a damp coolness rose up at me. The darkness thickened farther back in the huge cellar, and in it I could hear some of the men moving about. There were clinking sounds and smothered voices. An unfamiliar smell hung in the air, cold and cloying, a mixture of leaf-mould and cheap scent. I walked cautiously down the staircase. Now I could see the big barrels that were stacked in the middle of the floor, and the racks along the far wall in which masses of dusty bottles lay. I was in a wine-cellar.

As soon as the picture made sense to me, so did the sounds that I could hear, the glug and gurgle of liquid and the noises of human satisfaction. I called, 'All right, you can leave that wine alone. I want you all under the staircase here.' The wall beneath the steps was bare. 'Come on, I won't tell you again.'

The men came trooping out of the darkness, all of them beaming with happiness, each of them holding a bottle. Trower, pausing to raise his bottle for a swig, said, 'It's all right, corp, just this one to lay the dust.'

'It's a bit early in the day for that,' I said. 'You can do the first turn. Smithy—' this was to a man who was pouring wine down his throat at a rate that alarmed me. 'You go with him.'

The two sentries went upstairs. I said to the rest of the section, 'If you want to stay down here, leave the wine alone. Make yourselves comfortable where you are, and if anyone's got the idea of taking another look round, he can forget it.'

They settled down in a row against the wall, their knees up. MacAra (my lance-corporal) and I sat facing them, our backs to the stacked wine bottles, as grim as a pair of guards. For a half-hour we watched them like a couple of cats eyeing a large family of mice; but these mice were both venturesome and vociferous.

One of them got up and tried to saunter past me.

'Where'd you think you're going?'

'Can't a chap stretch his legs?'

'Not back there, he can't.'

'That's the sort of thing we're supposed to be fighting against,' he muttered in an injured tone, as he sat down again.

One of the other men stood up, and began to clash the crowns of two steel helmets together, like cymbals. 'Welcome to the Band of 'Ope,' he cried. 'Foller the Salvation Corporal an' 'is Saintly Lance-Jack an' 'Eaven will be your garden!'

The Roundheads against the wall filled the cellar with a great, pious shout of 'Alleluia!'

'Why should you drink the purple poison?' the orator went on. 'Ain't yer leadin' a life of 'orrible idleness, marchin' yer feet orf, gettin' stung by them 'eavenly mozzies, diggin' 'alf Italy up, swallerin' a 'undredweight o' dust a day, an' the nice 'ealthy sunshine fryin' all the fat orf yer? Ain't yer been wallerin' in luxury an' debauchery, wiv yer plates 'eaped 'igh wiv bully beef an' biscuits, an' processed cheese once a week, an' a pint a day o' that lovely chlorinated water ter wash yer troubles away?'

'Alleluia!'

One of the congregation began to sing, in a trilling soprano, 'Yield not to temptation, For yielding is sin…'

The chorus was taken up with fervour, the section displaying grins of blissful fatuity in face of the wooden countenances of the two NCOs.

'We'll have the next two for guard, I think,' I said. 'Take 'em up, Mac.'

MacAra took the next two men upstairs. He came down alone. Smith and Trower remained in conference with their reliefs for a few moments, then they came down the steps. Smith was swaying dangerously, and once he nearly toppled over the edge. Trower helped him down to the bottom, and settled him against the wall. 'Touch of the sun,' he explained to me in an amicable voice, and uncorking his water-bottle, gave Smith a long swig. Smith uttered a sigh of content, smacked his lips loudly and fell asleep. Then Trower had a long drink himself.

Silence settled upon the cellar. The men lolled against the wall. I could not tell whether they were dozing or watchfully awake. After all, they had already drunk a bottle of wine each.

As the silence continued, comfort and complacency settled upon me, and my eyelids grew heavy. Time crept by. A sound intruded into my doze. I opened my eyes. The sound continued. It was the hollow noise of an empty bottle rolling over the flagstoned floor. From behind the racks, on the far side of the cellar, came a scuffling. I was sure I heard whispers and frantic cautionary sounds. I got up, and just as I was on my feet, there was a catastrophic crash of collapsing bottles in the gloom. MacAra and I rushed behind the racks. There, on the floor, amid a litter of broken bottles and collapsed shelving, were the two sentries. One of them was just sitting up, still clutching a bottle by the neck. The other was on all fours, groaning. Behind them we saw the explanation for their presence—another door to the cellar, slightly ajar.

We dragged the two sentries, who were in a vinous stupor, back to their comrades, posted two more men, bolted the second door and rolled barrels against it until a battering-ram could not have opened it.

'I suppose this was your work,' I said to Trower. He smiled at me. 'And I suppose you two got a skinful yourselves,' I said.

'I shouldn't wonder,' he answered mildly.

Another half-hour passed. Some of the men slept, the rest muttered among themselves. MacAra took two more men upstairs to mount guard.

A few minutes after he had returned to my side, one of the sentries poked his head in through the doorway and roused me with an urgent shout. 'Corporal!'

'What is it?'

'You're wanted up here'.

I said to MacAra, 'Keep an eye on this lot,' and ran up the steps.

'Hey, corporal, quick—'

'What's up?' I asked the sentry. For some seconds after I had stepped into the street I was dazzled by the sun's glare.

'The officer—' he said. He sounded breathless.

'What officer? Get a hold of yourself, man!'

He pointed along the street. 'Him up there. He dashed off round the corner. He yelled, "Where's your NCO? I want your NCO." I don't know where he's got to now. He went off round the corner.'

'On his motor-bike,' the other sentry added. 'He yelled, "Come on, come on, get a move on!" Didn't he, Fred? I shouldn't hang about if I was you, corporal.'

A couple of hundred yards away was the corner they had indicated, where a side street turned in behind the first cluster of houses on the edge of the village. I hurried in that direction. I reached the corner, and could see no one. I walked down the side street, halloo-ing. I turned back. MacAra came galloping round the comer. 'What's up?' he panted.

'What'd you mean, what's up? And what the hell are you doing here?' I was feeling hot and bothered, and I sounded hot and bothered.

'What the hell d'you reckon I'm doing here? You sent for me, didn't you?'

'What d'you mean, I sent—?'

We broke off this mutual interrogation, stared at each other for a second, and both started running.

The sentries stood impassively in front of the door, gazing guilelessly to their front. 'I'll see to you afterwards,' I gasped, and rushed in through the door.

The section were in among the wine-racks, drinking happily from upraised bottles, rummaging, overturning, smashing, singing, shouting.

'All right,' MacAra shouted, 'the party's over.' The bawling and crashing continued undiminished.

I yelled, 'Upstairs, all of you, on the double. You've asked for it.' More war-whoops, snatches of song, and shouts of 'Alleluia!' 'Salvation Jack!'

MacAra tried to take a bottle from one of the men. The man resisted. MacAra hit him, and he landed on his back amid a fresh shower of breaking bottles.

'There,' MacAra said, as he hauled the wine-stained victim to his feet— the crash had silenced everyone in the cellar for a moment, 'You can report me for that. Striking a subordinate. Anyone else come funny and I'll do it again.' He let the man go and sent him lurching towards the steps. 'Come on, let's have the rest of you, now.'

We pulled the bottles from the men's hands and bundled them towards the steps. There were fuddled protests. Somebody said that they would all get sunstroke. 'That'll save me a lot of worry,' I said. 'You should have thought of it before.'

Some of the men lurched up the steps, some staggered. Some went up in couples, supporting each other. One went up on all fours, and one fell over the side of the staircase and stunned himself. They were all more subdued now, and full of boozy goodwill, all of them trying to tell us in thick, liquorous voices how tenderly, how paternally they loved their two NCOs, how we misunderstood them, and how sober they all really were.

We got them out into the open and the sunshine felled them. A couple were sick immediately. Others lay about, silent or groaning.

MacAra surveyed the scene of devastation. 'You going to bring any charges?' he asked.

'How can I? Can you see me standing up in front of the Old Man telling him about this?'

By now the men had all dragged themselves to the wall, where the overhanging roof cast a narrow strip of shadow. Trower and Smith had taken off their water-bottles and were passing them round.

The sentries, who were only slightly less drunk than the rest of the section, were looking more and more stricken. Trower said, 'Here, have a pull of this,' and handed them his bottle. They both drank deeply. Then, suddenly, one of them fell flat on his face. The other sank down on his knees, shook his comrade and implored him to get up, then burst into tears.

MacAra picked up the water-bottle, tasted, pulled a face and passed the bottle to me. 'Grappa,' he said. Grappa is a ferocious spirit made from grape-skins after they have been squeezed of wine. 'Not much we can do with them now.'

Blazing heat, empty stomachs, two or more bottles of wine each drunk by men who had never drunk wine before, and the final swig of grappa had finally floored the section. They lay scattered about as if a shell had burst among them. Even the two sentries were now prostrate.

There was only one thing to do. MacAra and I dragged all the bodies into a neat row, along one side of the building where we hoped that the occupants of any passing vehicles would not notice them, and then mounted guard ourselves. And there we stood, an hour later, miserably watching out for some officer to arrive and get us both reduced to the ranks, when the relief party arrived, with only—fortunately—a corporal in charge.

Apart from telling him not to laugh too soon, we maintained a dignified silence in face of his ribaldries, and helped him and his men load our section on to the truck. A few of our men had begun to recover, and staggered to the truck themselves, but none of them—not even Trower—could climb aboard unaided, and most of them had to be slid on like logs.

'Well,' said the relief corporal. 'There you are! Hallo, where have all my chaps gone?'

I pointed at the open door of the wine-cellar. 'I told you not to talk too soon,' I said. 'So long!'

For a half-hour the truck bounced and lurched along the torn, rutted road. The men in the back, unsheltered from the sun's glare, were squirming in a heap like worms in a fisherman's pot. With each sway of the truck they rolled and thumped from one side of the floor to the other, grabbing, threshing and kicking at each other, moaning, crying out, protesting, quarrelling, and from time to time hauling themselves up the side-boards, to hang over and be sick like landlubbers at sea.

The truck slowed down. We were approaching the company's camp. On our right ran a dry-stone wall. Behind the wall was a field of parched, brown grass. A peasant cottage near the wall had been chosen as HQ, a gap knocked in the wall close by to admit vehicles, and camouflage netting put up overhead to make a little transport park. Piles of gear were stacked outside the cottage, and fatigue men were trooping back and forward carrying things. The field was empty, but on its far side, concealed from air observation by an olive grove, the company were digging their shallow pits and making all their various preparations for a stay of unknown duration.

The truck turned in through the gap in the wall. The sentry gaped at us, then yelped, 'Here! Look! The dead cart!'

The fatigue men saw the section heaped in the back and took up the joke with shouts of, 'Bring out your dead!'

I was terrified that the noise they made, and the gathering crowd, might bring one of the officers out. I implored the driver to take us straight across the field to the olive grove.

'Sorry, corp,' he answered virtuously. 'This is as far as we go. I'm not allowed to make wheel-tracks across the field.' (This was another safety measure against air observation.)

The truck stopped outside headquarters. The section lay in the back. I sat hopelessly in the driver's cab, with the field, looking vast and empty as the Sahara, between us and the sheltering olive grove.

And now, a few yards ahead of us, the company commander was standing, tall and impassive, with his swagger stick tucked under his arm. I decided that I was within approximately ten seconds of the end of my career as an NCO.

I sat and waited for the end.

Then, from behind me, there was a thumping and a shuffling. I turned round. Trower had risen from among the heaped bodies, like a corpse from the common grave, and was lowering himself over the back of the truck. He reached the ground and stood there for a few seconds, clinging to the truck for support. He grinned at me, and in a corpse's voice said, 'Oh, ye of little faith!'

Then he began to walk across the field.

I got out of the cab and watched, spellbound, what followed. One by one the men stirred into life, crawled to the tailboard, heaved themselves over, steadied themselves, and began to stalk across the field.

One, two, three—I could not believe what I saw! They were performing a miracle, and it was for MacAra and me; for they, the lowest form of military life, had nothing to lose.

They were all on their feet now, strung out across the field in a wobbling single file, walking past the company commander one by one, all of them silent, all of them looking straight to the front, all walking with the stiff, perilous stride of clockwork toys. The films have shown us what zombies are supposed to look like, and that is what my section looked like, crossing that field.

One by one they reached the olive grove, and as soon as they were in among the trees they pitched to the ground. The officer watched them with a calm, impenetrable expression. I took my heart in my hands and followed. As I passed the company commander, he called, 'Corporal!'

I halted, ready for the worst. 'Yes, sir?'

'You've got a good section there. Look after them.'

I went on my way.

I reached the olive grove, with MacAra at my side. The men had crawled into the shade of the trees and were settling down to sleep, with their heads on their packs.

I said, 'We'll have to wake 'em up later, to get dug in.'

'Plenty of time,' MacAra answered. He opened his pack and took out a bottle of wine. 'Our share,' he said. 'I reckon we've earned it.'

He put the bottle to his mouth, drank half its contents without stopping for breath, wiped the neck of the bottle on his sleeve and passed it to me. I tilted it up and drank the rest of the wine. Soon we were asleep among our men.

Chicolino

The fighting in Sicily ended suddenly as far as we were concerned. In effect, it left us behind. One night, filthy and tired after thirty hours on the move, we lay down to sleep in an olive grove with batteries of twenty-five-pounders banging all round us. The next morning we woke up and everything was quiet. The sky was clear and blue. The guns had limbered up and gone off, leaving a litter of cartridge cases among the vineyards. The whole British Army seemed to have passed us by in one night, for the roads were empty except for an occasional lorry that roared past, like a repentant straggler, and vanished in a cloud of white dust.

Several days passed, and we remained where we were. It was uncanny. There was fighting going on at no great distance from us, for we received daily situation reports on it, but we could not hear it. There was only the vast quietness, the occasional mumble of invisible aircraft in the sky, the deserted roads, the sun burning the air and darkening the vision with its glare, and our bemused selves—we might have been the only soldiers left in the world—prowling about and making friends with the peasants. Many of the soldiers began to put forward the theory, which they embraced with a childlike fierceness, that we had been forgotten, mislaid, as it were, by the army, and that we might stay here for months before 'they' got their hands on us again. This idea cropped up so often, and was clung to so bitterly in the face of all previous disappointments, that it was clearly the expression of an unquenchable secret hope.

We were happy. Peasants came to trade eggs for corned beef, or to ask for medical care. Occasionally a soldier would arrive, a lonely pilgrim, 'deserting' from a hospital or reinforcement camp back to his unit, the only place he could feel secure. He would receive food and shelter and go on his way.

One morning a boy walked into the camp. He wore a shirt and shorts of khaki, and a big-peaked Afrika Korps cap. At five hundred yards he looked like an enemy, but at a hundred yards we could see that he was an Italian boy, thirteen or fourteen years old.

We were lining up for breakfast. He approached to within a few yards of us and paused, watching us warily.

Sergeant Craig, who shared a tent with me, called, 'Hi, come here, Chicolino. Don't be scared.'

The boy trotted across to us, his diffidence gone, a lift of bravado now showing in his stride. He greeted us with a broad, impudent grin and a loud, 'Hello', the 'h' sounding gutturally in his throat.

'Hungry?' Craig asked, '*mangiare?*'

'You bet. Plenty.'

The sergeant broke his two mess-tins apart and gave the boy one of them. 'You get in line here behind me.'

'Okay.' Again the flashing smile.

'Where'd you learn English?' Craig turned and spoke to the boy as we shuffled in line towards the cookhouse.

'*Soldati.* Me all the time with *soldati. Tedeschi. Canadese.*'

'Germans, eh? And Canadians. Busy little feller, aren't you?'

'Sure.' The boy answered without understanding. '*Canadese* good. *Molto mangiare, molti sigaretti, molte caramelle.* Plenty.'

Our mess-tins filled, we squatted in the shade of an olive tree. Craig and I watched the boy wolfing his food. After a while he lifted his head and grinned at us.

I asked, 'Where are you from?'

'With *soldati.*' He waved his hand at the plain on which the battle had been fought.

'Your home?'

He pointed at the hills. 'Misterbianco.'

'Are you going back? Returning? *Tornare?*'

'No go back.' His answer was fierce. 'Fight there. *Battaglia.* Boom. Boom. No good.'

'Your family? *Mamma? Pappa?*'

He shrugged his shoulders. '*Me ne frego. Scappare.* Run away. *Mamma, pappa, bambini,* all go from home. Boom. Boom. Bomb. Yes? Bomb. Run from home. In hill.' He pointed again. 'Me no *bambino.* Me no stay *mamma, pappa.* Me no take food *bambini.* Night, me *scappare,* run. Me with soldiers. Good with soldiers.'

His story was not a novel one. We had often come across boys, some of them tiny little waifs of six or seven, who had become detached from their families and who wandered across the plain like little prairie dogs from one group of soldiers to another.

I said to Craig, 'Misterbianco should be clear by now. I'll see what today's sitrep says. We'll take him back.'

'No.' The boy had caught the sense of my words and spat the refusal at us like an angry little animal. 'No go back.'

'We'll see about that.'

There were only rumours about Misterbianco that day. We decided to wait until the next day's official situation report came through.

Throughout the day the boy followed us about the camp. He walked with a happy swagger, and grinned impudently at everyone else as if advertising the fact that he was under our protection. After breakfast I sent him to the well for water and made him wash himself. I gave him a comb and he tore at his gleaming, curly hair until it was tidy. We gave him Craig's spare shirt and shorts to wear, and put those he had discarded in a can of water, boiled them, scrubbed them and hung them on a branch to dry. At lunchtime we lay outside our tent smoking, enjoying the feeling that we had a servitor, while Chicolino— as we continued to call him, although he had told us his real name—took our place in the cookhouse queue and brought our food back with his own.

He chattered to us all day about his adventures with the Germans and the Canadians. The Canadians had taught him to swear in English, and he did this with enthusiasm. He spoke of the Germans so raptly and innocently that they might have been a favourite football team. He did not seem to be aware of any difference between the Germans and ourselves. They, and we, were soldiers, the same species; that was all; and he reported their doings to us as if he had been deputed to carry news from one branch of an accidentally divided family to another.

Evening came, and with it the problem of where Chicolino was to sleep. There were no spare blankets, and we could not leave him out in the open, for the area was infested by malarial mosquitoes.

We were occupying two-man tents; Craig and I decided that we could make room for the boy between us. We had two blankets, one of which we used beneath us and the other as a covering.

We told Chicolino that he was to sleep with us.

'Sure,' he answered, with a sly grin and a confiding drop of the voice. 'I go with you. You good fellers. No go other *soldati*.'

Craig and I went into the tent, took off our boots and anklets and pulled the blanket over us. Chicolino crawled in through the triangular entrance and knelt on the blanket at our feet. He slipped off his shirt and let his shorts fall to his knees. He stood up, kicked them away and went down on his knees again. Kneeling there, pale and slender in the transparent darkness, he had a posture that puzzled us faintly, the graceful and compliant posture of a girl crouching on a bed. He looked from one to the other of us with a hesitation that we still did not understand; then he lay down between us, turned towards Craig, and lifting his face voluptuously, put his arms round Craig's neck. He uttered a few words, in Italian, in the pigeon murmur of an amorous girl.

I was sleepy, half-turned away, hardly taking in what was happening. Craig's angry snarl of surprise roused me. He leaped up out of the blankets, blundering about in little booming collisions with the wall of the tent, tore open the flap, bundled the naked boy out and threw his clothes after him.

'Did you ever see anything like it?' He was muttering to himself, releasing an intensity of feeling that I had never seen in him before. 'Did you see that? The dirty little tyke! Did you see it?' The words were sticking in his throat. I could see the film of sweat gleaming on his face. 'The idea! The little devil! See what he thought we were after?' Apparently it was less Chicolino's actions than what the boy had thought to be in our minds that angered him. 'He deserves to be—. What can you—? A kid of that age? It's past believing!'

We could hear the boy outside stumbling about among the guylines, and the flapping of his clothes as he dressed. He was sobbing.

I asked, 'What can we do with him?'

'Shoot him for all I care!'

We sat up and looked at each other in the darkness. I wanted to go out to the boy, but I felt shy of going out alone. I guessed that the same thing held the sergeant back. We rose together, pulled our boots on and went out of the tent.

Chicolino was sitting on the bank of a nearby irrigation ditch, dangling his legs. He turned his head and watched us come up to him.

I said to him in my limited Italian, 'With us there's none of that.'

He took no notice of my words, but peered up at me with his face screwed up in an embittered expression. He muttered, 'Why did you treat me like that? What had I done to deserve it? Don't you care for me?' His voice, like his expression, was sulky and aggrieved.

I translated for Craig's benefit. 'I told you,' I went on. 'With us these things don't happen. Wrong.'

'Wrong!' Chicolino shrugged his shoulders derisively and shaped his mouth in a disbelieving pout. 'The Germans cared for me. Canadians cared for me. Ah,' he burst out. 'The Germans were good. They were beautiful. They were tall and strong, and they were as brave as devils. They were not afraid of the English. They laughed at the English. They did not run away from the English. They went away to fight elsewhere. Ah, the English!' He filled his mouth with saliva and spat. We could hear the breath quickening and catching in his throat, and see the tremor in his shoulders as he was seized again by the smart of rejected affection.

We did not know how to talk to him. In our middle twenties, we were both too innocent of life to understand him. Any kind of morality was as incomprehensible to him as to a young animal. He did what he had been taught to do, and it was natural to him. All the ardour, the still blind affections, the unshaped impulses of his years, had been directed into a wrong channel, and the torrent of his feelings filled him with its force, making him strong and bitter and impregnable against our words. It was impossible to chasten him, only to hurt him. All we had done in throwing him out of the tent was to outrage him. We did not know what else we could have done. We, too, were bewildered, outraged, upset. We stood over him helplessly.

Craig pointed to the tent. 'Get in there.'

'No.' The boy made an obstinate, coquettish gesture with head and shoulders.

'Come on. Don't be a fool.'

'No. You don't want me. I shall find others.'

Craig gripped him by the shoulder and raised a threatening hand. 'Get in there.'

The boy cringed away from him like an animal and crawled into the tent. We followed him.

'Here.' The sergeant's voice was still angry. 'Take this.' He pushed one of our two blankets across to the boy.

I said, 'And keep your clothes on. We always do.'

Chicolino took the blanket, rolled up in it and turned his back to us. Craig and I pulled the other blanket over us. For the rest of the night the three of us lay still. I do not know if the other two slept. I did not.

In the morning Chicolino was a boy again. He ran about as if the sunlight had touched him with a beneficent magic. He washed himself and proudly showed us his clean neck, went for our breakfast, scoured our mess-tins out for us, smoked the cigarettes we gave him and looked us in the eyes without constraint, as if no memory of the previous night remained with him.

After breakfast he went into the vineyards to pick grapes for us, while we went to our officer. The lieutenant gave us the morning's news, agreed that it was safe to go to Misterbianco and gave us permission to take the little platoon truck.

We found Chicolino and told him that we were taking him home.

He put down the helmet full of grapes that he was carrying.

'No.'

'You must go home to your family.'

'No. It is not safe to go to Misterbianco.'

'It is safe now. Our officer has said so.'

'I do not come from Misterbianco. I was lying.'

'When we get there we'll find out if you were lying.'

'You cannot take me. I shall go away from here.'

'You'll go to Misterbianco with us.'

He seized Craig's forearm with both hands. 'I beg you, let me stay here. I want to live with the soldiers. I am happy with the soldiers. Let me stay.'

Craig looked at me, and I repeated, 'You've got to go home.'

Without warning Chicolino darted away.

I shouted, 'Catch him!' Several soldiers closed in on him and brought him back to us.

We lifted him into the truck. I climbed in at the back with him, and held his arm. The sergeant drove.

When we were going at a fair speed I let go of Chicolino's arm. I spoke to him several times during the journey, but he would not answer. He sat as if he were going to prison.

The road climbed and twisted as we drove up into the hills. Nearing Misterbianco, we passed the scene of recent fighting. Cottages were ruined, burned-out vehicles were tipped into the roadside ditches, and the clusters of graves, British and German, grew larger and more frequent.

For the first time Chicolino took an interest in his surroundings, gazing around him with a frank, appreciative expression as if he were enjoying a visit to a museum. Once he pointed, and said, 'Look, there are some English dead, unburied. Four. Let's stop.'

'Why?'

'I think a machinegun did it, the way they're lying. I should like to see.' He spoke in the bright voice of a boy telling his father how his toy aeroplane works. 'Besides, they may have cigarettes in their pockets.' He looked at me, clear-eyed and hopeful.

I did not answer.

He looked forward again, along the road we were travelling, and saw houses. He fell silent once more, and hunched himself up in his former wooden, brooding posture.

Misterbianco was in sight. We were climbing the last stretch of road. There was a field on our left, sloping uphill for about three hundred yards and ending against the skyline in two small knolls. At the verges of the road stood signboards in English and German warning that the field had not yet been cleared of mines.

Craig slowed down at the last bend. He turned in his seat. 'There it is.'

I said, 'Drive right through till we come to a square. There's—'

Chicolino leaped over the side of the truck.

I yelled, 'Come back!'

We stopped the truck, as Chicolino plunged through the barbed-wire fence and ran across the minefield.

We followed as far as the wire, and stopped at a yellow signboard with a black skull-and-crossbones on it. Craig was calling, 'Stop! Stop, you little fool!' I was shouting, 'Mines! *Mini*! *Pericolo*!'

The boy ran on across the field and we waited, numbed, for him to blow up. Unharmed he reached the dip between the two knolls and paused there.

He turned and looked back at us for a few seconds. We called after him, and heard our own voices floating uselessly on the heatwaves as if someone else was shouting. He turned away from us and trotted over the hilltop, going away from Misterbianco, down into the far valleys, passing finally out of our sight.

The Desert Mouse

'The Highland Division?' said Sergeant Craig. 'Don't talk to me about the Highland Division.' He sipped his beer and frowned. 'Oh, I don't know, they were all right, I reckon. You know what their only trouble was? Too much publicity. I suppose the name was what you might call romantic. None of these here war correspondents ever seemed to know about any other lot. Well—' He emptied his glass and signed to the barman for another. 'Wasn't the Jocks' fault, I suppose.

'Still, in those days—'forty-two, 'forty-three, the desert, Sicily, seems like a dream now, doesn't it?—in those days we used to get hot under the collar about it. Wherever there was Jocks there was trouble. The fights I've seen between them and chaps from other mobs! Cairo, Tripoli, Syracuse, Catania—you only had to be in a bar with plenty of liquor laid on, and pretty soon the tables 'd go over and the bottles 'd start flying. Who started it? Six of one and half a dozen of the other, I reckon. I remember one time in Catania when chaps from Fifty Div—now that was a crowd if you like. Nothing in the world to touch 'em—was going round in gangs challenging every other bunch of fellers they came up against in the street. "What Div?" If the other lot answered, "HD," or if they had it up on their sleeves—wallop! So you see, it wasn't all their fault.

'Still, I was going to tell you. This time I was at the convalescent depot at Ionia. There was a big sergeant there, a Jock from the Black Watch, and he never gave us any rest. He was bumming his load all the time, jeering at our mobs, bragging about his own. We were a bit fed up, I can tell you.

'Still, no one did anything about it. We were sick and tired of him all right, but what the hell, we were all on the sick list and nobody wanted to start any trouble. I might as well be honest about it, a bashing off this Jock would have been no joke. Real Gorbals he was. He said he could fight dirtier than any man living. Well, that's what he said.

'Then one day he started shouting about the Seventh Armoured Div. I remember we was all sitting out in a garden at the time, enjoying a nice peaceful afternoon in the sunshine.

'"Desert Rats," he says, "they should hae called 'em the Desert Mice."

'He was that sort, this Jock, if they get hold of something and they think it's funny, they won't give it a rest. So there he was, red in the face with his own joke, and he kept on and on about the Desert Rats being a lot of mice.

'In the end another sergeant gets up out of a deck chair. He's a stocky little chap, none of us 'd hardly noticed him before, he never usually said a word. Well, he walks over to the Jock, past me, and I noticed he had the Rat up on his sleeve.

'Everyone shut up. You could 'a heard a bloody pin drop. The only thing you could hear was the studs of his boots smacking down on the concrete.

'He stood right up to the Jock. It looked a bit comic. He was half a foot shorter, at least. Then he says, very quietly, "Just you say that again, what you said."

'The Jock looks at him for a minute, and lets out a bloody great roar of laughter, and he says, "Why, lads, here's the littlest wee mouse ae 'em all."

'We just kept quiet.

'The little chap says, "Shall you and me take a walk?"

'The Jock doesn't answer for a minute. Then he says, "Well, sergeant, I'll tell ye—" and all of a sudden he lets fly with his boot, quick as lightning, to take the other feller by surprise.

'But the little feller slips out o' the way like a flash, and then right off— bang, bang! Talk about the old one-two! The little feller lets him have it right in the guts, and as he doubles up, he smacks a terrific left hook into his chin.

'And then, rat-tat-tat. Talk about the bloody postman's knock. I've never seen such fast punching in all my life. It's no surprise afterwards when this little sergeant tells us he's a professional. There's the Jock going over, and the little feller must 'a hit him half a dozen times on the way down.

'Thump! It's all over bar the prayers. The Jock's on the floor, with the other feller standing over him.

'"The trouble with me," the little feller said, just as quiet as before, "I can't take a joke. I buried too many of my mates."

'And he lifts up his bloody great hobnailed boot and he brings it down, right on the Jock's face.

'"A souvenir from the Desert Mice," he says, and he walks back to his chair.'

The Indian

There is often as little similarity between an incident in real life and the same incident as it appears in a story as there is between seed and flower.

I think of this whenever I look through my novel *There's No Home*. The central story in this book is of a love affair between a British soldier and a Sicilian girl in nineteen forty-three. Both are married and are long separated by war from their married partners. They keep apart for some time after their first meeting, out of loyalty to their own ties, out of respect for each other and because of a vague, unexpressed disgust for the orgy of promiscuous love-making that is going on around them. Finally they come together; and the scene in which this happens is an uneventful one, without drama. They are sitting together, they are talking, they run out of words, they look at each other in silence, they become aware of the tension between them, they rise to quit each other's company—and the girl, who has hitherto been the more stubbornly resistant of the two, suddenly clutches the man's hand and leads him into her house.

I think it is a good scene. But whenever I read it there rises from some depth of memory the thing that really happened; and it strikes me how much more complete, more dramatic, more revealing of character the real incident was than the written one. Put them side by side, ask the reader to choose which was the seed and which is the flower, and he would almost certainly choose wrongly.

This is what really happened.

The soldier and the girl were sitting outside her house in a little slum street, talking. They had spent several evenings in this way, recovering from the heat of the day, enjoying the mildness of the sunshine, eating almonds and laughing at the silly jokes which are so delightful when one is young and in love. The girl was nursing her baby, and she seemed to be sheltering behind it from the man's desire. From time to time their conversation would lag, and they would become aware of the strain between them, as they had been on previous evenings, but neither of them was yet sufficiently resolved to act. Each time they fell silent they would exchange fierce, hasty glances, quickly averted, and would quickly break out into talk again.

They were scarcely aware of what was going on around them. The noises of the street were dream noises, a flow of babble, clatter and chatter to which they half-listened as if it were a pleasant but unregarded music. It was not the noise which, late in the evening, roused them from their mutual absorption, but a sudden break in it. They both sat back, wondering, for the air had emptied of the continuous hubbub and a silence was flooding into the street, driving before it a confusion of shrill screams, the panicky clacking of wooden sandals on the pavement and the slamming of doors.

A woman rushed past, crying, 'Gl'Indiani,' and vanished into her house.

They looked away to the end of the street and there, swaying in the middle of the suddenly emptied roadway, was an Indian soldier.

At that time, in the late summer of nineteen forty-three, there were Allied soldiers of several nationalities in Sicily, gathering for the invasion of the Italian mainland. Most of them were on the best of terms with the people; particularly the American negroes. I doubt if any of these young coloured soldiers had ever been as happy as they were at this time. The Sicilians did not look on them with any racial consciousness. There was neither aversion nor that self-conscious generosity towards them which is as offensive as hatred: simply an instinctive leaning towards them, as if out of recognition that the same ardours, simplicities and secret depths of temperament, fostered in both of them by centuries of savage sunlight and slavery in the fields, existed in them both alike. The women loved them, not out of the insulting oversexed greediness which had drawn many women to them elsewhere, but simply because they were the gayest, the finest-looking and the most unfortunate of all the poor devils in uniform whom the war had cast upon this island.

It was the very opposite with the Indians. Why, I cannot say, for they were also fine-looking men, slighter of physique, often mild and classically handsome of countenance, but bearing themselves well and generally behaving with a more mature courtesy than any other troops I have ever seen.

The British soldiers loved them, and called them 'proper gentlemen', the highest of tributes. They kept to themselves. Sometimes—I do not know whether it was because they were not used to wine—we saw some of them drunk, but although drink sometimes made them childishly sportive, they were never maddened by it, and I never saw any of them made ill or swinish by it as our men sometimes were. We used to watch them washing themselves, fascinated by the ritual scrupulousness of their ablutions. We accepted their cleanliness as a symbol of their self-respect. It was strange to hear their shrill chatter as they walked past us; it was like the overexcited chatter of children; and it seemed strange to us because we knew that they were the bravest of men. It was generally believed—whether with justification I cannot say— that they were used more prodigally than British troops, being regarded by authority as more 'expendable' than pink-skinned soldiers, and we looked on them with all the more sympathy.

But in spite of all the praise that we had for them, I never saw them accepted by the Sicilians. Instinctively, unreasonably, the people feared them. Perhaps some ancient superstition was at work, some ancestral Mediterranean fear of the men from the East. Whatever it was, it was a fact that a couple of Sikh soldiers had only to come walking, quiet, dignified and absorbed in their own conversation, along a street, and civilians would give them a wide and fearful berth, while women snatched their children indoors.

The Indian came lurching down the street, doors banged and the street emptied. The soldier and the girl realised that they were alone, watched by many pairs of eyes from black, barred windows.

The girl rose, clutching her baby to her, and moved to go into her house. The soldier caught her arm and drew her gently back to her chair. 'Sit down,' he said. 'He won't hurt you.'

The Indian halted and looked about him in a vague, drunken puzzlement. He crossed to a closed door and began to bang on it with his clenched fists, crying out in a language that neither the soldier nor the girl could understand. The girl said, 'He is a devil. Let me take my baby inside,' but the soldier's restraining arm kept her in her place. 'Listen to him,' he said, mystifying the girl with the pity in his voice; for she was too frightened to recognise, as he did, that the Indian's cries were not threatening but appealing; her dilated eyes could not see how lost and lonely the lithe, dark-skinned little man along the street looked, as he thumped imploringly on a closed door.

The Indian saw the couple and came towards them. The girl looked up at the soldier, silently begging him to let her go. Holding her arm he could feel how violently she was quivering. She could have torn herself from his grasp, but it was his will that kept her where she was; it was her animal acceptance of his will, a first implicit recognition of shared fates.

The Indian halted in front of them, and she pressed her baby closely to her, bowing her head so that her face lay almost upon the child's.

The soldier said, 'Hallo, Johnny. Having a good time?'

The Indian uttered a high-pitched laugh of delight and repeated, like a pleased child, 'Hallo, Johnny.'

The soldier smiled. 'Too much wine, eh?' He mimed drinking, then whirled his forefinger round. 'Like this, eh? In here.' He tapped his head.

The Indian beamed and nodded his head rapidly. 'Noggood, noggood.' He clasped his head on his hands and closed his eyes.

'Makes you sleepy?'

The Indian responded with more violent nods, and cried, 'Yess, yess. Yess, yess. Vairy slippy.' He leaned over the baby. The girl sat rigidly, her eyes upon the face of her soldier as if crying out for some recognition of her courage in not shrinking back. 'Preddy baby,' the Indian chirruped, touching the baby's face with his fingertips.

The soldier said to the girl, 'Dice "bella bambina".' She flickered a tight-lipped but momentarily brilliant little smile, then lowered her eyes again.

'Your lady let me hold baby?' The soldier could see that the girl, although her eyes were downcast, was listening to the reedy sing-song of the Indian's voice as intently as if she were trying to understand unfamiliar music.

'I'll ask her. Have you got babies?

'T'ree. I got t'ree.' He held up three fingers. 'Me married when litta boy.' He held up fingers to indicate thirteen years.

'How old are you now?'

Again the Indian held up fingers. Nineteen years.

The soldier told the girl in his halting Italian. 'He is only nineteen years old. He was married when he was thirteen. He has three children.'

She looked straight at the Indian for the first time, her eyes wide with interest. Her lips were still compressed in doubt.

The soldier said, 'He wants to hold the baby.' She shrank into herself and her eyes flared a refusal.

'Don't be frightened,' the soldier said. 'You've let me hold her. He knows how, better than me. Here, give her to me.'

She hesitated, then handed the baby carefully to the soldier, not daring to disobey him. She clutched her hands together as if regretting what she had done.

'Here!' The soldier handed the baby into the arms of the Indian, who at once began to chick and chuckle with delight, rocking the little girl skilfully in his arms. He hummed a tune, a strangely high-pitched and broken tune, and dandled the baby happily. 'Ek! Ek!' he cried. 'She smile. Look, she smile!'

The soldier smiled and looked at the girl. She, too, smiled, her face filled with relief.

'Give her back.'

The Indian obediently handed the child back to the girl.

'I got to go,' the Indian said. 'Now I go, back to compannee. Go to slipp.' He shook hands solemnly with the soldier. The girl rose from her chair and, holding the baby in the crook of one arm, held out her free hand. The Indian shook it with grave formality. He cried, 'Chirr'yo,' and left them.

For the first time, as they watched him walking away, the soldier and the girl noticed that the other people had come out of their houses and were watching from their doorsteps. None of them shrank back as the Indian passed them, but they looked at him as they might look at any passing stranger, and their talk shrilled noisily across the street once more.

A little later the girl put her child to bed and came out to sit again in the street. For a while she and the soldier remained silent. They were both full of their own thoughts, unwilling to utter any more trivialities, yet closer together in the silence that united them than they had ever been before.

The soldier spoke. 'You are a good girl. You were a kind girl to let him hold your baby.'

She looked at him, and he saw that her eyes were full of kindness. '*Ti voglio tanto bene*,' she replied. 'You are a good man.'

It was that night that they became lovers.

Mrs Grocock's Boy

I do not think that Raymond Grocock knew he was in the Army to kill other men. I doubt if it occurred to him that other men were out to kill him, even when they were trying to do it. Once upon a time he had been happy in the Boy Scouts; and the same thing—being able to dress up and pretend he was having adventures—was happening again.

Among the rest of us he was half-butt, half-pet. He was the sort of boy whom workmen send to the storeroom for a handful of rubber nails or a left-handed screwdriver. In all our doings he was the timid and admiring onlooker, hovering on the outskirts of the group, with his great tired mop of hair, his old-man's face, seamed and leathery, and his anxious eyes. No amount of drill had been able to rid him of his stoop, to prevent him from always cocking his head to one side, or to remove the fixed, wondering grin from his face. He preceded everything he said with a prolonged 'Aaah', while he collected his wits; and as he did so, the effort of thought made him squint behind his steel-rimmed spectacles.

He came from the Potteries. In his appearance and in his speech there was all the ugliness of his birthplace. His body and soul, both sickly, gave the impression of having been smoked like bacon in factory fumes. He was the only son of a widowed mother, and he had lived most of his life in her kitchen. He told us about the meals she cooked for him, the books that he and she read to each other, the games of snap that they played, their weekly trip to the pictures, and the nights when his 'aunties' came visiting. He had worked as a labourer in a glassworks; it was clear from the way he talked that his days in the factory had not played much part in shaping him. He must have been quite alone among the other workmen, chaffed by them, helped by them, as he was by us, but apart, like a child among them, trotting gratefully home to his mother at the end of each day's work.

A child in a man's body he remained, although he had been in the Army for two years. His flesh grew to the proportions of maturity, but his soul refused to grow up. In the end he was to grow up—that is what this story is about. The shape of his life was to be recast in an hour; and terribly.

For what eventually befell him I still feel guilty, although I was only one of many who were responsible. In our attitude to him we veered between kindness and a hobbledehoy cruelty; and I know now that it was the kindness that struck him down; the old tragedy of good intentions, of unpredictable consequences, of the darkness in which we all walk. Everybody was in it, from his fellow privates to the company commander, and pity was our treacherous counsellor.

For instance, he should never have come to Sicily with us. There were intelligence tests before we sailed. Those who failed to pass were transferred to home service units. Raymond failed. But he went to the company commander—there really were tears in his eyes—and begged to be allowed to go with 'the boys'. The company commander took pity on him and consented, God forgive him!

Yet Sicily did not hurt Raymond. He never really understood what was going on. It must have been like being allowed to join the gang of big boys on the street corner. The big boys were playing adventures, and he was allowed to go about with them.

His greatest joy, at this time, was to be our errand boy. He would trot away on a commission, a broad, greasy grin of bliss on his face, his lips visibly working as he repeated his instructions softly for fear of forgetting them. I remember him, during a halt in a terrible march, running about in the vineyards to pick grapes for his comrades; sitting with a home-made rod and line by a stagnant, malarial pool in a river-bed because the men had told him he could catch fish there; going a couple of miles to the water-truck; staying up all night to watch over a sick man; happily lending his pay to all comers; and once, in Catania, being sent to a brothel to ask for a bottle of Maid's Water.

The respect he showed his NCOs was embarrassing. Nothing unnerved me more surely than the awe-struck grin with which he watched while I showed the section how (for example) to deal with a booby-trap. I lived in dread of his, 'Eh, yow doan' 'alf know some clever things, corporal.'

I sometimes tried to imagine what the fact of his absence meant to his mother. After all, he was happy enough. He had fallen headlong into an exciting dream (for all this, like being at the pictures, was not real to him). But she—how stunned, how incredulous she must still be, that some stranger had had the power to take her 'baby boy' away from her. It would not have disturbed her that all the other young men had gone. There had to be soldiers. They were part of the scene, like lamp-posts. But that the vast sweep of the net had scooped up her Raymond with all the others must have seemed an act of lunacy, an error as big as the universe, an atrocity (as indeed it was) that made the whole of mankind a collective war criminal. Day and night she must have lived from one freezing spasm to the next of fear and incomprehension. For her, too, life must have become a dream, but a bad one.

Yet, contradictorily, when his letters came she would feel pride. He would tell her how well he was getting on, and she would feel the same surprised pride as she had when his schoolmaster had sent an encouraging report, or when she had seen the other boys letting her Raymond play football with them. She would say to herself wonderingly, perhaps aloud, so unbelievable it was to hear the words, 'My Raymond is in the Army. *In the Army!*' When she saw big, sunburned soldiers walking past, she would think, 'My boy is one of *them!*' She would stop her neighbours in the street and tell them the latest news from him; and numbed, as if in a dream, she would hear them referring to 'Mrs Grocock's boy in the Army.'

Towards the end of the Sicilian campaign Raymond left us. He was taken away with cerebral malaria, a dangerous form of the disease which leaves its victims seriously weakened, sometimes mentally impaired, and usually unfit for further active service.

The fighting in Sicily ended. We rested. We crossed to southern Italy and hung about in transit camps. Weeks went by without our being employed, and the rumour spread that we were going back to England. It was the same ridiculous rumour that was always spreading among the troops. This time it was true. The company commander confided in the company clerk, who confided in the whole company. It was the end of November, and our sailing date was in the first week of December.

Three days before we were due to sail, Raymond Grocock dropped off the back of a lorry and dragged his kit into company headquarters. He was yellow with illness, more stooped and stupid than ever. The clerk asked him for his papers. He mumbled 'A'n't got none. I run away from that place.'

More questions elicited the fact that 'that place' was a transit camp to which he had been sent from hospital to await posting to a new unit.

Perhaps this was the second crisis at which we failed him; for if he had been sent back to the transit camp he would have been found a light job somewhere for the rest of the war. But he looked sick and helpless, and it seemed so much the merciful thing to take him back to England, although we all knew why we were going. Besides, his return seemed as mysterious and miraculous as the homing of a dumb animal. This lumbering child, weakened and more befuddled by illness even than he had been before, had shown the courage and intelligence to escape from a guarded camp, had wandered for days across southern Italy, had found his way, had dodged the Military Police, had got lifts, had begged food and shelter. He squinted anxiously at the company commander. 'Let me stay with the boys, sir.' The officer listened to the hoarse, imploring voice, sighed, and said, 'All right. I guess I can fix it. Report back to your old platoon.'

That was how Raymond became one of the thirty thousand 'picked men' whom Montgomery brought back to England to lead the invasion of Normandy.

Four and a half months went by between the end of our disembarkation leave and our departure for Normandy. They were the most strenuous training period we had ever known. Almost every day there was some moment at which Raymond should have been weeded out. But by now, for the whole company, it had become a matter of habit to help him. Poor wretch, he had been slow enough before, but now, with his brain affected by the malaria, he was like a punch-drunk boxer. I once saw a gelignite charge explode dangerously near to him; he only lowered his head and blinked. When we went to sea practising landings he was ill and useless. There was another intelligence test, at which he failed. There was a medical examination, at which he was down-graded. Yet he remained with us.

By now he had become such an institution among us that none of us was capable of *seeing* what we were laying up for him. We felt complacently virtuous when we thought of him. We were flattered by his gratification whenever we helped him. It was enjoyable to feel protective. We liked to have him running errands for us. We thought we were being humane, but it was not really as a human being that we treated him now. He was our mascot, our regimental goat. Human qualities can petrify and degenerate: our kindness had turned into something unpleasant.

On June 4th several score thousands of men swarmed aboard a fleet of ships in the Solent. Their appearance was warlike, their manner in general subdued. They were going about a serious business: to breach the walls of the greatest fortress in history. Our company was among them. Each of us had his own preoccupations, and nobody stopped to think how it was that Raymond Grocock, a lamb to the slaughter, came to be among us.

At sea he was a great nuisance. Most of us sprawled about the decks in thoughtful silence. He, on the contrary, was a picture of idiotic energy; running up and down ladders to explore the mysteries of the ship; coming up to us—always with that ghastly grin on his face—to tell us what he had found; continually bobbing up in front of me, all feverish and anxious, to ask me if his buckles were done up correctly, or how soon he would be allowed to eat his assault ration, or if I reckoned we would see ourselves on the newsreels. Once, when I was busy over a map with the other NCOs, he sidled up to me, attracted my attention with a conspiratorial leer, and asked me furtively if it was true, what one of the men had just told him, that they had girls in France who let you see them with no clothes on.

On the evening of the 5th I lost sight of him. I was grateful for the respite, but began to wonder where he was. Walking about the decks, I found him. He was lying face downwards by the rail, horribly seasick. He turned his face up to me. It was a lost, frightened child's face. Seasickness was something he could not account for. He had the stricken appearance, the resentful eyes of a small boy who is being punished without being told what for. When he spoke, it was in an exhausted whisper, as if he had spewed all the eagerness out of himself. 'What we stopped for, corporal?'

'Waiting for the word "Go", I suppose.'

'Well, why don't they start? I feel ill.' He spoke in a ridiculous, resentful, serious voice, as if the state of his stomach was something that must be reported at once to the General Staff.

'That's too bad, boy. You'll have to grin and bear it.'

'But I feel ill.'

'Shut your eyes and go to sleep.'

I did not hear what he mumbled in reply as I left him.

I slept soundly until the alarm bells rang at dawn. We washed, had a scanty breakfast and assembled at our boat stations. Most of the men were quiet, still heavy with sleep. Raymond was unwashed, his hair tousled, the front of his tunic stained with vomit, his face a sick buff colour. His equipment was hung about him in a silly muddle. I told him to put it right. He gave me a vague, drugged look and did not move. Bowie, one of the other riflemen, took hold of him and rearranged the equipment as a mother tidies her child's clothes. Raymond stood passively under the movements of the other man's hands. I asked him if he had slept during the night. He answered with a half-hearing shake of the head.

The rest of the men busied themselves tightening each other's belt buckles at the back, fitting each other's packs tight up between the shoulders. Raymond stood apart from them, one hand resting on the ship's rail, looking out over the sea with a puzzled expression. He seemed to be wondering where he was. Once or twice I caught him looking my way. Each time, his mouth would open, and clefts of effort would appear beside his nostrils; then there would be a blink of resignation, and the resolve would fade from his face.

We went down into the landing-craft. When Raymond's turn came he looked at me again, like a dumb animal imploring to be understood. I tapped him on the shoulder and said, 'Down you go, soldier.' He lowered his head and obeyed.

Our journey to the shore began. There must have been a lot of noise. I cannot remember it. Noises seemed to lose themselves in the vast openness of sea, shore and sky. We were sealed within our own soundproof thoughts. I stood in the bows, on the track of a self-propelled gun, watching the distant strip of beach.

Behind me the men were quiet. I looked back. Raymond was squatting against the steel bulwark, as limp as a sack. His expression was entirely empty.

I looked out over the bows again. The beach was plainly visible, a thin strip cutting the sky with wavy dune-lines and the squat sharpness of villas. It was undramatic and untidy. Men were toiling ashore and crossing the beach in little files. All their movements seemed slow.

Someone tugged at my sleeve. It was Raymond. "Ere, corporal. I want to report sick.'

I could not have taken this in, for I turned away from him again. Then I turned to look at his face again, and I realised what had attracted my attention. The face, twisted in its wheedling grin, was as empty as before, but the eyes glared entreaty. 'Please, corporal—' The horrible thing was that his voice was so calm. '—I want to go sick.'

The thing was too unreal to reach me. 'Go back to your place and be a good boy.'

'I want to see the doctor. I don't feel well.' His voice had risen, but there was no more in it than the shrill nagging of a child denied his wants.

The landing-craft was turning slowly, pushing through the inshore swell. The world was all beach now. Wrecked landing-craft lay broadside on. Pyramids of stores grew at the water's edge. The swarming of men had the same mysteriously purposeful confusion as the turmoil of a disturbed anthill. The Channel behind us was like Columbus's Atlantic, its far shore beyond imagination; and we, with chilled hearts, waited as our little steel shell, cut off from all the rest of human kind, wallowed in the last troughs of water towards the touch of hard sand against its hull, towards our unknown New World. And, coming between me and this world, the idiot voice nagging in my ears, 'You take me to the doctor. I know my rights. If I want to see the doctor you got to take me.'

Nothing had happened to provoke this from him. Our progress had been uneventful. No dreadful sights had shocked us. He haunted me, like a creation of fantasy, breaking up the image of the real, vast, violent world ahead. 'I'm not fit. I can go back if I want to. I shouldn't be here by rights. I'm a light-duty man, I am. The doctor in Italy told me. He said full duty was too much for me. I can change my mind if I want to. You send me back. I want to go back.'

I turned on him. 'For God's sake, shut up!' I had no time for pity now. Bowie took him by the arm and pulled him back to his place.

I clambered again on to the track of the gun. The water around us now was thick with rubbish, which clung to our bows. I could hear Raymond, among the silence of all the other men, moaning complaints incessantly like a child. 'I'll report you, I will. You got a grudge on me. Why don't you take notice? I want to go back. I want an interview. You get me an interview with the Old Man. I know my rights.'

Ahead of us, a party of Ordnance men were clearing the beach of mines. They ran a criss-cross of instantaneous fuse out over the sand; their sergeant waved his hand, they threw themselves flat on the ground and he fired the fuse. The fuse exploded with a flash, and here and there mines were set off, throwing up domes of dark brown sand. The men scrambled to their feet and went on with their work; all except one, who remained on the ground wriggling like a cut worm, the victim of their sacrificial hurry. It was all obsessed and inhuman: antlike. And behind me, an absurd and inharmonious musical accompaniment, Raymond's voice. 'I'll write to my mum, I will. You wait till I tell my mum. They'll put it in the papers. I'll get you in trouble, I will. You wait and see. You're supposed to look after me. I'm not supposed to be here. Why don't you let me go back? Listen to me!' He screamed at my back, 'Listen to me!'

The beach was almost upon us. Not far away a pontoon ferry, out of control of its crew, drifted crabwise out of the marked safety lane. A cargo of petrol cans was stacked high along its deck. I watched, fascinated; for the men aboard were standing along the side watching disaster draw towards them, as idle, as apparently dissociated in their helplessness, as loungers at the rail of a seaside pier. The world for me, at this moment, was the sight of these men and the sound of Raymond's voice. In the moment that the ferry grounded there was a small explosion and a dab of flame; then a great white detonation from stem to stern; a flash like the sun; the men disappearing; the whole shape of the craft disintegrating; an enormous, many-coloured upboiling of flame and black smoke; burning petrol cans sailing through the air; the heads of one or two men bobbing in the water, swimming slowly to the shore; and Raymond—Raymond, burying his face in his hands, began to cry. It was not the sight of the explosion that made him cry. He was crying to attract our attention from it, back to himself. It was a loud, ugly crying, like a small boy's. It did not touch the heart, but aroused disgust; a demonstrative, recriminatory, howling demand for attention.

I was furious with him for demanding my attention, at this last moment of transition between lives. The tears were running down his face and he was smearing them into his cheeks with his hands. His hair was disarranged, his equipment in a tangle again, and green slime hung from his nostrils. He saw me staring at him and blubbered all the louder. His whole behaviour was a deliberate regression. He was throwing himself upon our hands, advertising his return to complete childishness, abdicating in the moment of crisis; for the yellow pennant at which we were to touch down was only a few yards ahead. All of a sudden the bill had been presented to him; he could not meet it.

Bowie leaned forward, pressed the cold muzzle of his Sten gun against the back of Raymond's neck and spoke into his ear. The effect was immediate. Raymond gave a last heartbroken snuffle and shut up. He remained in his place, his head bowed, utterly inert.

At that moment I heard a shout from the man beside me. There was a bump, a faint lifting of the bows as we rode on to an obstacle, and a sharp, not very loud bang. I remember seeing the steel deck open upwards in ragged petals, being lifted bodily from the track on which I stood, feeling myself in the middle of a slow revolution of earth, sea and sky, seeing the face of a stricken man staring up at me, feeling myself lying on my back (I remember no impact) with seawater freezing through my clothes, my eyes being dazzled by the bright whiteness of the sky, the seeming slowness with which torn pieces of metal swooped down out of the whiteness, and the boots of my section clattering past me. I climbed to my feet and ran after them, feeling angry because they had left me behind. I ran alongside them as they trudged up the taped path, and shouted something to my lance-corporal. Even immediately afterwards I could not remember what it was, nor hearing my own voice, but he told me later that what I had yelled, petulantly, was, 'Take the rear, Frank, I'm not —ing dead yet.'

As I passed the section I had an impression of Raymond moving forward a few paces with a slow, heavy step (I do not know how they had got him ashore); then stopping, and Bowie sending him spinning forward with a blow on the shoulder. After that Bowie kept him moving in this way, like a brainless inanimate toy, spinning and lurching along.

I cannot imagine why we did not leave him behind. Perhaps we still, without thinking, wanted to look after him, for we had been warned that the beach, ranged by the enemy's guns inland, would be an unhealthy place in which to linger. More likely it was the mere instinct of conservation, as if he were a property we did not want to leave behind.

We continued inland, unhindered except for occasional stray small-arms fire from distant clumps of trees which, upon orders, we ignored. A picture lingers in the memory: of my men, a long, extended file, moving in a slow, hunched procession against the cold white sky. Their bearing was slack, they looked interested in nothing but their burdens, yet collectively they emanated a vast wariness, for the whole landscape was a mantrap. And in the middle of this line, breaking its slow steady rhythm, being driven along like a slave in Egypt, was the will-less, shamed, stumbling figure of Raymond Grocock. Bowie continued grimly to thrust and cuff him along, but the other men ignored him; and if he had, at that time, any consciousness of what was happening to him, this must have been the worst of it. Absorbed in their own slow steady progress, the men had shut him out of their consciousness. A glance, turned his way, would sweep across him as if he were not there. Voices clashed over his head in little snatches of conversation. If he obstructed someone, he was thrust aside gently, without interest. It was macabre. He walked like a corpse lifted up from the grave by the scruff of its neck. He might have been invisible to all the section except Bowie. From time to time he raised his head, glared about him like a prisoner and muttered to himself in an obsessed, persecuted monotone.

By the afternoon we had reached the field where we were to stay the night. We sat down on our packs, took time off for a smoke, then set about a familiar routine. We spread our damp blankets out to dry, put mess-tins of water on our tommy-cookers to boil, cleaned the clogging wet sand and dust from our rifles and began to dig our holes in the ground. The men paired off to dig, each couple working turn and turn about. Each man, in his free spells, brewed tea, cleaned and greased his boots to preserve them, cooked and ate some of his assault rations, washed and shaved. Later, if we were lucky enough to remain 'stood down', we would get into our pits and sleep.

Life was becoming comprehensible again. As our mood changed, the men began to take notice of Raymond once more. With the irritant of danger removed, they saw him again as he had been—their friend, their pet.

But for Raymond there was no going back. He sat on his pack silent, sunk in himself. Men wandered across to him, slapped him on the back; tried to cheer him up, offered him sweets and cigarettes. They told him that there was nothing to worry about now. Beneath their rough jocularity there was an anxious note, as if they were pleading with him to forgive them for the last few hours. Raymond only glared up at them with brief, black glances.

Meanwhile, Sergeant Craig and I had gone to talk with our officer. The lieutenant wrote a few lines in his message pad, tore the page out and gave it to me. 'Send Grocock down to the Aid Post with this. They'll ship him back to England as a casualty. He'll be better off out of it, poor devil.'

I walked back to Raymond and held out the note like a peace offering. 'Here you are, Raymond, boy. Your troubles are over now. Here's your ticket home. You're a lucky old chap. I wish I was coming with you.'

I was naïve enough to expect him to relax, to look relieved. Instead I saw the most concentrated look of hatred and misery I have ever seen on a human countenance. He backed away from me.

Bewildered—for I had just witnessed a transformation which I could not yet understand—I advanced a pace or two, still holding out the note. 'Here you are, Raymond. You've only got to take this to the Aid Post. They'll look after you.'

His eyes were fixed on my face. Without shifting his glance he reached out and took the note from my hand. He did not say a word.

The men were crowding round him, congratulating him on his good fortune. Their manner was mild, anxious. Each of them was trying to ingratiate himself with Raymond. He stood up and swung his pack over his shoulder. He stood there, looking about him as if at bay, and what had happened to him became plain. From this moment to the end of his life he would be an old and bitter man. The skin of his innocence had sloughed off him. His boy's dreams had been blown away. He could not pretend anymore. He had grown up: and in humiliation. And we, because we had been the witnesses of this, were enemies in his eyes.

Men called out their friendly good-byes. He stood there, between two trees, looking at them, pouring hatred out upon them.

The voices followed him. 'So long, Raymond.' 'Good luck, boy.' 'Give my love to your mum.' Bowie stepped forward and said, 'Here, Raymond. I'll walk down with you. Let me carry your pack.'

Raymond backed away, shifting his pack behind him as if to protect it from Bowie. I was the only one close to him, and I was the only one to hear the words—the horrible, illuminating words—that he muttered. 'I hope you die. I hope you all die.'

For we were the witnesses of his exposure. As long as a single one of us survived he would be the prisoner of his shame. He slunk away through the trees, followed by the boyish, friendly cries of farewell.

Daisy May's Crew

We were enjoying a dreamy day in the country. We walked along a deserted lane that wound, white and rutted, between rustling unkempt hedges. The roadside cottages were decayed by time, leaning on each other lopsidedly as they sank into the soft earth. With their uneven roof-slopes, their rough indefinite outlines and their grey softness of colour, they did not stamp themselves against the pattern of the fields but hid in it. Their shadows met to make of the village a little patch of tranquillity beneath the wide arches of sunlight.

Muffled detonations could be heard from time to time through the heavy stillness of the summer air; for this was Normandy; but the sounds of war were less potent than the warmth, and we disregarded them.

We rounded a bend in the lane and came face to face with a tank. It filled the roadway from hedge to house. We stared up at it like urchins: a massive beast of steel crouching between its tracks, looking down at us along its depressed gun barrel.

The tank was unattended, but from within the house we could hear men's voices raised in dispute, the shuffle of boots and a heavy bumping noise. We slipped sideways past the sleek steel flanks, seeing the name white-painted on the turret above us: *Daisy May*. We came round the rear of the tank and saw its crew. They were emerging from the doorway of the house, and between them they were carrying an upright piano.

The village had been deserted by its inhabitants. Many soldiers had passed this way and the houses had been stripped of everything movable; everything, apparently, but this piano; and now that, too, was going to war.

The four men staggered out into the road, each stooping beneath the weight of his corner of the piano. They were shouting the usual confusion of advice at each other. 'Your end up a bid' 'Round to the right!' 'To me!' 'Easy on, Charlie!' There was a discordant jangle of strings and the piano was lying on its back across the rear deck of the tank.

Their sergeant said, 'Have a blow, lads,' and they lit cigarettes. He saw us watching and grinned at us agreeably. Tall and sunburned, with his black beret on the back of his head and his shirt open to the waist, he looked as if he were taking a tractor to the harvest, not a tank to the regions of death. We had seen many tanks pass along this road and few return, and from the surviving crews we had heard of the slaughter that the armoured divisions were wreaking on each other only a few miles away. I wondered if the sergeant knew of this. He must have known, for we had seen tanks of his unit going to and from the forward area in the last few days; but his smile was unshadowed, and his voice was sturdily happy as he jerked a thumb at the piano and called to us, 'Come in handy, this will.'

When the tankmen had finished their smoke they lashed the piano down to the deck, working swiftly and expertly together. They climbed aboard and the tank moved away along the lane like an earth-ship. We listened to the dull roar of its engine and the scuttling noise of its treads as they came running unendingly back towards us.

One of us called, 'Enjoy yourselves!' The sergeant, poised in the open turret, raised two fingers in reply. The tank slewed round the bend. For a long time after its body had vanished from sight we saw its turret travelling above the level of the hedgerows, the long gun barrel at rest and the sergeant looking steadfastly across the peaceful landscape towards the firing line.

Mélanie

I first saw Mélanie on a summer night in Normandy, in nineteen forty-four.

My company was resting in an orchard. All round the edges of the field the men had dug shallow pits in which, each wrapped in his single blanket, some enjoying the additional comfort of looted bedding, they were fast asleep. The night was warm and clear yet heavy with a sweet fullness, as if it had gathered into itself all the ripeness of unharvested crops and unpicked apples that made the battlefields so deceptively fair, a wasted richness that was itself a desolation. Aircraft murmured in the sky, but the anti-aircraft guns were silent. Artillery flashes flickered and briefly stained the night, showing up with their radiance the gentle undulations of the fields; but even the noise of the guns had somehow become absorbed into the quiet, so that we were no longer aware of it.

Around the edges of the field our sentries lurked, a pair in the shadows near a gap in the wall, another pair leaning up against a tree so that they were part of its black bulk in the darkness, another prowling along the far end of the field. I was the guard commander, inspecting the sentry posts from time to time and drowsing in the intervals among the off-duty men.

At about three in the morning I roused myself and set out on one of my tours. I was still heavy with sleep, dreamy as I walked, and as I passed along the line of pits and looked down at the huddled sleepers I felt that I was still with them in the bottomless world of sleep. In sleep they were less like soldiers than like children in their cots, their attitudes defenceless, their faces vacant or revealingly sinful or frightened.

A patch of bright colour gleamed in one pit. It was unaccountable, something that my drugged mind, checking dully on the list of familiar things which was all it could encompass, was unable to explain. I stood on the parapet of the trench and came fully awake. The colour was yellow, a daffodil yellow, strangely soft and gleaming. I leaned forward and saw that it was a silken quilt. It was a beautiful quilt, out of place in this open grave. Well, I thought, it was more useful here than in its owner's bedroom.

But I did not move off. Something about the sleepers under the quilt had caught my eye. One of the two faces, strong and darkly weathered, I knew. The other face was white and thin, and about it spread a mass of blond hair, thick strands of which fell across the face of the other sleeper. I stooped lower. Yes, it was a girl. She and the soldier were fast asleep under the quilt with their arms about each other, as still and innocent as babies.

Whatever my duty might have been, I did not do it. I walked away. The sight had been so innocent, so natural, so subtly comforting that I accepted it as a relief from the feeling of sleepless drudgery, of suppressed fear, of bodily uncleanness that had burdened us all for days. It was not until later that I was able to feel even faintly surprised at the discovery of a woman among this huddle of verminous males. The villages round about were battered and deserted, their inhabitants sent back to safer places in the rear. Military police guarded the roads to stop civilians from wandering into the forward area where they might endanger themselves and become a nuisance. How she had got here I could not imagine, and though I made her acquaintance later I never found out. That Eldridge, her sleeping partner, had been the one to find her was less of a surprise, for he was one of our authorised characters, a completely lawless but quiet-voiced ruffian, a hard drinker who could always hold his liquor, a Military Medallist and a man who could find in the most unpromising surroundings anything that he needed for the maintenance of human comfort.

We were lucky enough to stay in the same place for a couple of weeks, and as long as we were there, Mélanie—within twelve hours the whole company knew her name and spoke of her as if she were an old friend— stayed with us.

She did not remain Eldridge's property. It did not occur to him to make any claim to her. She had breakfast with him and drifted quietly away from him like a little wraith, and like a wraith she moved among us in the days that followed.

She was short and sturdy, but more shapely than most of the thick, brawny Norman girls. Her fair hair was dull and dirty, and no womanly vanity ever moved her to comb it or put a ribbon in it. She wore a dirty white blouse and a short black skirt. Her bare legs were scabby. She washed her hands and face, but nobody ever saw her perform any more extensive toilet.

Yet, if she looked ill and dirty, we were not repelled, for she only seemed all the more of our world, the world of those who swarmed dirty and forgotten beyond the boundaries of civilised living, the world of violence and suffering. As she moved among us, an impulse of scarcely recognised affection moved among us, too, touching our hearts with little pressures of pain.

Men fed her, and some of them slept with her, but she was never insulted and those who refused her never did so in any way that might offend her. I remember, too, that I never heard anyone joke crudely about her or speak of her with contempt; although, certainly, no one spoke of her or looked at her sentimentally. It did not occur to anyone to pity her. It was simply that she was accepted. In all the essentials, she was one of us.

I think she washed clothes for some of the men; and, when she was permitted to, she would cook a meal. She always looked vaguely frightened; she never laughed, though she sometimes smiled, wryly and appealingly. She rarely spoke, and when she did her voice was scarcely audible, with a tone of fright in it. What was she frightened of? Not of us, nor of the occasional overreaching shell that fell hereabouts, nor of the more frequent air attacks. She paid less attention to these than we did. I saw her once, when a German fighter had just streaked overhead firing its cannon and was turning in the distance, perhaps to return. She was standing quite still under a tree, her face uplifted as if in wonderment. Men who had tumbled into their holes called to her, and she looked at them as if they had disturbed her thoughts; then she seated herself, squatting on her heels and drawing her skirt out primly over her knees, beneath the tree.

She should, of course, have been sent away, to one of the civilian reception areas. Nobody thought of doing so. The NCOs accepted her as their men did. The officers must have seen her but none of them ever spoke to us of her, and when one of them appeared she would vanish silently, as if warned by instinct.

I remember one morning when two of us were cooking breakfast. She stood before us—where she had come from we did not know—and greeted us as sedately as a little girl. We said, '*Bonjour*, Mélanie,' and invited her to sit down. My companion broke out his mess-tins and gave her one of them. We shared our ration of sausages among the three of us and ate without speaking. Then, into the same fatty mess-tins I poured tea, and all three of us drank.

Afterwards, I said, 'Cigarette?' She thanked me politely and took one. The sun was shining and the three of us stretched ourselves out contentedly, smoking in silence. I remember how all my muscles, which had so often been contracted with suspense that it sometimes seemed as if they would ache for ever, relaxed, merely because there was a girl lying between us, and how consoling it was to look sidelong and see her gentle profile turned up to the sky.

After a while she said to me, '*Tu viens avec moi?*'

I answered, 'No thank you, Mélanie,' feeling a little ashamed as if I had refused a proffered kindness.

She asked my companion. He looked at her for a few seconds, then shook his head, smiling at her.

The three of us drowsed together for a little while longer. She rose, and thanked us for the meal. I asked her if she wanted another cigarette. 'Not now,' she said. 'I shall see you again.'

She walked away, and soon afterwards we saw her making her way across to the barn, walking calmly and unhurriedly on her own, with two soldiers following a few paces behind.

I am convinced that it was not a naked sexual hunger that drove her. She did not behave like an oversexed woman; later on I was told by men who had been with her that she had been a passive lover. She did not give herself for gain. She asked us for nothing; all she had from us was food; and she knew well that most of us would have fed her whether or not she made us any return.

What impulse, what instinct kept this girl among us? I am sure that no process of thought was involved, that she acted as mindlessly, as assuredly as an animal. Was it some dumb working of the great force of feminine love, or of an even wider loving-kindness? Was it fellow-feeling, misery reaching out to misery? Are there some women who are drawn to men within whom they can feel the presence of death? Or was it merely that she was dazed, frightened by the sudden transformation of all her known world, afraid to leave what was perhaps the only place she knew, clinging to the security that the presence of men offered and ready to remain with them on these fundamental, animal terms?

A few days before we moved out, the Field Security Police arrived in the area.

Their first activity was to search our camp for loot. They found nothing, for while they were paying a preliminary visit to our headquarters, our company commander sent his sergeant-major out by the back door to warn us.

After that they searched the wrecked village for civilians. They found Mélanie in a barn and drew her out, a shrinking frightened little creature in their midst. In a ruined cottage they surprised us by finding another civilian, a great, black-bearded fellow in a workman's blue blouse. They questioned him on the spot and told us before they left that he was harmless, a Paris factory worker who was on the run from a German forced-labour round-up and who had been hiding in the village, uncertain of what was going on around him and afraid to come out into the open. It appeared that a number of other men from his factory had already come into our lines, some of them bearing credentials from the Resistance Movement, and he had been able to give correct answers to questions about them.

He and Mélanie were told that they must return with the policemen to a safer place. As the party walked away to the jeeps that were waiting for them, Mélanie smiled palely at the soldiers and some of them, watching at the gap in the wall, smiled back and called kindly farewells. As she walked away she slipped her arm up through that of the big man next to her and he, accepting her, let her clutch his forearm with her little hand.

That was the last we saw of her, holding on to the arm of the stranger like a little girl with her daddy.

Being and Non-Being

It was one more halt in one more Norman village. Files of men clattered into the farmyards, broke up and sank to the ground in sprawling khaki groups. We ignored our surroundings, for we were all dog-tired. We were in that state where a week ago is too far back to remember. We felt as if we had been badgered and herded about all our lives, always dismally sure that at the end of each heartbreaking task another would be waiting. Time, and with it reality, had broken up into a succession of irregular spells of sunshine and rain beneath which we lived unsheltered. We never had any consciousness of place, for wherever we wandered, we always seemed to be in the same field, with the same untidy hedgerows cutting off our view. I lay inert, with no idea of the absurd but significant encounter that awaited me here.

Orders were given and groups of men moved into the surrounding fields and orchards. A guide led my section through the apple trees to the edge of a high bank overlooking a lane. We put down our packs and began to dig. Picks rose and fell in a resigned apathetic rhythm.

I left my partner to make a start on our pit, and went off foraging. I spoke good French, and could always be relied on to bring back eggs, brandy and vegetables, so that the division of labour was a happy one.

I walked down the village street, looking into the broken, deserted cottages. There was a two-storey building at the crossroads: the post-office. The high garden wall at the back was broken down in several places. The building, too, was damaged, with part of its upper wall blown away and one slope of the roof caved in upon the gap. I went in, past the counter, to a large empty kitchen. The floor was littered with plaster from the ceiling. I stepped through a broken doorway into the garden and clambered over the rubble of a collapsed outhouse.

A woman was standing in the garden. I asked her, 'Where is everybody?'

'Gone away.'

'Why did you stay?'

'I preferred to wait for your people.'

'But the bombardment?'

She pointed to a deep, timbered, German air-raid trench behind her. 'I spent two days down there.'

'All the time?'

'Yes.'

'Did you have food?'

'At first. I was too greedy to make it last.'

'That was the cold. Didn't you feel it, at night?'

'I had a blanket. But it was horribly cold.'

'Weren't you frightened?'

She lifted up her left hand and showed me a book. 'I had this.' She smiled. 'I must look filthy.'

'Don't worry, you're in the fashion.'

She came past me, a scarecrow, her dress limp and soiled, her hair dishevelled, her face masked with grime.

'Let's go inside.'

In the kitchen, I stretched myself out in a wooden armchair, enjoying the sensual pleasure that the ache of fatigue affords when it flows through a relaxed body. She took a broom and began to sweep the plaster away.

She had left her book on the table. I picked it up. It was a volume of Paul Valéry's poems. 'Do you read this?'

She turned to face me, leaning on the long broom. 'You seem surprised.' She studied my face, and laughed. 'I understand. But you know, I'm in disguise. I didn't look like this two days ago. And you? You speak French well. Have you read them?'

'A long time ago.'

She laughed again. 'Now you must permit me to be surprised. One doesn't expect it of a soldier who walks into a ruined house with a *mitraillette* under his arm.'

I touched my face. 'Perhaps we should postpone this discussion till I've shaved. Do you live here?'

'No. I was visiting. I am an official of posts and telegraphs. My husband is in Paris. I was on a tour of duty, but as you see the war caught up with me.'

'Why did you stay, then? Didn't you want to get back to your husband?'

She shrugged her shoulders. 'Neither of us will grieve.'

After a few seconds, she went on. 'You know, it seems ridiculous, but it was a consolation to read those poems while I was in the trench. It was a refuge. Do you know *Le Cimetière Marin*?' Her face lit up with pleasure and her voice quickened as she went on to speak about the poetry. Clearly it was a joy for her, all the more because the chance was so unexpected, to be able to talk of such things after her ordeal. Her mind, as numbed and cramped as her body by the nightmare confinement in the trench, was stretching itself and coming back to life.

I was not paying attention. Phrases came to me, but I did not even try to grasp at them. She was talking about the lucid music of words, the machine of language with its own non-human logic, the philosophy of pure form. In the fetid darkness of the trench, with the giant tread of bombardment trampling upon her senses, she must have dreamed herself away into an abstract, lyrical world. It was the most enviable faculty of the educated, in times like these, the power of escaping through the mind, so that they could often remain serene when others had to flinch with animal panic or—if they were sound enough—to endure with animal stolidity. Where others came to terms with the beastliness and chaos of the living world, changed within themselves to fit it, and even grubbed in it for the primal satisfactions that alone made life bearable, they were able to reject it.

As for me, I was unable to respond. Four years of my life had already drained away in uniform. Content to live physically active and intellectually lethargic, at the new level, enclosed in a womblike warmth of comradeship, literally unaware of past or future, I had let every thread of connexion with my old life snap. Now that, in these fantastic surroundings, I had the chance to think and to talk about things I had once cherished, I did not want to. My interest in them was dead. The woman's chatter meant nothing to me and the desperate eagerness with which she spoke, as if seizing at some staggering and precious opportunity, seemed childish. I had evolved into a different kind of animal, preoccupied at this moment with only two things: to enjoy physical repose and to study the female beast of my species that stood close to me. She was thin and dirty and at least ten years older than me; and I was tired. She was asking me if I knew the line about the universe being 'nothing but a flaw in the purity of Non-Being'. I stood up and said, 'I've got to go now.'

'Already?'

'I'll come back later.'

She followed me to the door. 'Listen.' There was a desperate little ring in her voice. 'There's a bedroom upstairs. You can share it with me tonight if you want to. I won't disturb you. It'll be better than lying out there in the orchard.'

'You shouldn't stay in the house. Wrap yourself up and stay one more night in the trench. This place isn't safe yet.'

'I'm too tired to care. I'm going to sleep in my bed tonight. Stay if you wish. All that frightens me is being alone.'

I had no active desire either to stay or to go. I was tired, and the simplest thing was to plod away on my rounds like a toy that had been wound up and started off on its course. 'Thank you. But I'm in charge of a section, and they are digging in, over there in the orchard. I have to stay with them.'

She did not answer or give any sign of disappointment, but came to the door with me and stood watching me as I walked away.

I had only gone a few yards when my company sergeant-major came out of another doorway and walked along with me. He was a quiet, solid man who kept up the minor courtesies whatever the surroundings. 'Good evening, corporal. Yon's a nice lassie you left at the door. I dare say you could get yourself an invite if you tried.'

'I've had one, sar'-major.'

'Didn't you fancy her?'

'I fancy a night's sleep in a bed.'

'What's stopping you, laddie?'

'My section's up in the orchard.'

He halted, and laid his hand on my arm. 'Who's your lancejack?'

'Frank Chase.'

'Och, let him take over. He's a reliable feller. I'll tell your officer I've kept you down here. You go on back to her, now. I shall know where to find you if you're wanted. Go on, boy.' He spoke gravely and sincerely, without any man-to-man doggishness in his voice. 'Sleep soft when you can. You'll feel the better for it. Away now!'

The woman made no comment when I returned. She was still leaning against the door-post. She stood aside, compressing her lips in a wry welcome, let me pass and followed me into the house.

We did not talk about Paul Valéry during the evening. We swept out the kitchen and restored the furniture to some kind of order. I fixed the loosened shutters back into place as well as I could. We collected timber and started a fire in the hearth, filled a big cauldron at the well in the garden and dragged it in to heat over the fire. When the water was hot we washed our bodies down and soaked our feet. We dried ourselves in front of the fire with the small, rough towel from my pack. I shaved, and we dressed. I had come away from the orchard, bearing in mind the possibility of barter, with some tinned rations in my pack. She contributed some ersatz coffee and cooked a meal. We ate the hot food with a feeling of transcendent gratification; and afterwards we smoked, silent and contented.

Without haste we went up to the bedroom. It was in the part of the upper storey which had not been hit, but one of the window frames had been blown out, together with some of the surrounding bricks, and the usual layer of ceiling plaster covered the floor and bed.

We swept the floor, shook out the sheets and made up the bed. The woman pulled her clothes off, standing at the foot of the bed. She was not ill-looking now, with her hair combed back and her sharp little face, intelligent and sympathetic, turned towards me. I hardly noticed her. I took off boots, trousers, tunic and jersey and lay down on the bed in my shirt and underclothes. In that strange world, this was for me the imaginable limit of undressing. I felt the bed sag as the woman stretched out at my side, recognised in the sheets the sour smell of builder's size, left by the fallen plaster; and was fast asleep.

I opened my eyes and wondered what had awakened me so quickly. The room was dark. There was an urgent clutching at my left arm which I could not, at first, account for. My watch, on the chair at my right, told me that it was four o'clock in the morning. I had slept for seven hours. I realised who was shaking me, and turned over, suddenly feeling the emanation of her warmth as I did so.

'I'm sorry,' she whispered, 'but I'm frightened. I had to wake you.'

After the sleep, my mind was clear again. I ached all over, feeling the same strange pleasure in it as always. The artillery was in full cry, the slam and thud of guns filling the night. Muzzleflashes seared intermittently across the gaping window-space, and each time they lit the room they showed me the woman's white face and her white shoulders emerging from the sheets.

I took her hand under the blanket, and she pressed it to her. Her body was hot but dry, and I could feel it trembling.

'Those are British guns,' I said. 'There's no need to be frightened.' All the noises of the night seemed to roar around the house, shaking it but failing to gain entry, so that our bedroom seemed like a little black cell of silence in which, however quietly we spoke, our voices sounded loud and unfamiliar.

'It's not the guns. It's the aeroplanes.' They were crawling about in the depths of the sky. 'They've been coming all night, dropping flares and bombs. I slept for a while, and then I woke up, and I haven't been able to sleep since. I've been lying here for hours, remembering that this house was right on the cross-roads, and frightened to death. I was determined not to wake you. I thought you must surely wake up with all the noise, but you slept. My God, how you slept! And in all that noise! They were overhead again just now, and I couldn't stand it any more. I started to shake you. Now that you're awake, they've gone away for a while, and you think I'm frightened for no reason.'

I put my arms round her and she came gratefully close. I asked, 'Do you feel better?' I could feel the movement of her cheek against my skin as she nodded.

I felt no more desire for her now than I had the evening before; only an elementary pleasure in her warmth, and the deep primal consciousness of human companionship in the weight, the movements, the pressure of limbs mingled with mine in the darkness. She was all bone—the sharp shoulders, the prominent pathetic collarbone, the hips and limbs. I could scarcely feel her limp, flat little breasts against me.

It was she who stirred, taking possession of me with sharp and urgent movements, assailing me in the darkness like a feverish little animal. For the first time, the weary absurdity of the whole episode came home to me, the accidental way I had drifted into it, the sergeant-major packing me off to her.

She uttered a little sound of release in her throat. A few moments later she whispered—this cultivated Frenchwoman, lying in a bare room, in sour stale sheets, against the half-washed body of an unknown man, with the flash and roar of death all around and death prowling the sky overhead in search of her—'All the same, this is better than the purity of Non-Being.'

A Pal's a Pal

I once heard an officer call Private Eldridge 'a good soldier of the old school'. I suppose the officers saw Eldridge as a leftover from the age of Kipling, with his drunkenness, his illiterate but invincible cunning, his physical strength and florid good looks, his whoring, his braggadocio and the boisterous courage that had earned him his Military Medal.

It was understandable that officers of the old school liked him and sighed for the days when there had been whole regiments of men like him; but most of his companions in the ranks hated him. He was no older than his comrades, but a spiritual gap of generations separated him from them. Part-tamed, part-strengthened by the education of elementary school and trade union, they despised his ignorance, his vices and his pitiless lone-wolf philosophy. They were too strained and indifferent, in that autumn of nineteen forty-four, to regard with any sympathy his ostentatious bravery.

At that time the left flank of the British armies was bogged down in the flooded lowlands of Belgium. The dash from France had petered out. As the days shortened, the dank chill and drizzle of Flanders ate into the men's bones. Their energy and enthusiasm drained away. The marks of war-weariness appeared on thousands of faces.

The Flemish towns and hamlets were crowded with shabby, tired soldiers, shapelessly bundled in jerkins, scarfs, stained khaki greatcoats and clumsy waterproofs. A few pockets of Germans held out along the coast, but they were content to remain hidden in their strongholds, and their besiegers were reluctant to do more than surround them. The flooded countryside was deserted. Along the straight, raised roads that intersected it, an occasional patrol might be seen trudging with sullen step, the slow bobbing pace betraying the fear rather than the hope of a hostile encounter. But when the lonely little cluster of men or the scudding vehicle had vanished, the silent landscape, under its infinite grey roof of cloud, seemed to speak of the inert exhaustion that lay upon both sides.

Parties of men were able to go to Ostend or Brussels for a few days' rest, and it was only during these interludes that they were able to feel any pleasure in living, or even any warmth in their flesh.

I was sitting one evening with Ted Trower in a dancing-bar in Ostend. The three-piece band was resting, and in its place a girl was playing the violin, to a piano accompaniment.

I was watching the girl. Trower was watching me. My face must have betrayed my fascination. I was enchanted—not by her face, which was thin, aquiline and grave—but by her attitude, so full of a grace that I had almost forgotten. Her head was bowed over the instrument, and the listening remoteness of her eyes, the slight flowing movements of her arms, the touch of her fingers on the strings, the relaxed stillness of her body, mirrored like ballet the sweet, gentle melodies that she played.

She finished, disregarded among the chatter, and I sent a waiter across to ask her if she would have a drink with us. She came to our table, inclined her head slightly in greeting, said quietly, 'Good evening, messieurs,' and sat down.

I was awkwardly silent for a few moments. Trower, after nodding to her, sat brooding over his drink as if signifying his withdrawal from the affair. I said that I had enjoyed listening to her, and she answered with a transient smile. I said that it was a pity she could not play in some place where people would listen. She smiled again and said, 'Where?'

'Have you always played in bars?'

'No. I was a music student at the Conservatoire in Brussels.'

'What made you give it up?'

She shrugged her shoulders.

'Why did you come to Ostend?'

She glanced negligently around the crowded room, without answering.

'Why don't you go back? I'm sorry, are my questions annoying you?'

'No, I'm not annoyed. There's no point in my going back.'

'But why not? You shouldn't stay here.'

Trower had been studying us both, and the ring of earnestness in my voice brought an amused, faintly pitying expression to his face. He said to the girl, 'Jewish?'

She faced him with a startled, suspicious look. 'Yes.'

'Family?' He had only picked up a few words of French, but he could use them, with differing inflexions, to make sense.

'All deported.'

Satisfied, he hunched over his drink again. I stared at the girl. At length, she said, 'I was seventeen when I saw them last. Three years ago. I was an only child. When they realised what danger we were in, they brought me here, and found a family to protect me, and left money for me. Then they went back to Brussels. After a while, their letters stopped, and I heard that they had been taken away. I have no one else. There is no point in my going anywhere, and it doesn't matter to me what I do.' She looked up sharply, and I turned to see Eldridge standing behind my chair.

'Nice judy,' he said. 'A'n't you going to ask a chap to sit down?'

'What are you after?' Trower asked. 'More ticket-money for the brothel?'

'Give us a chance,' Eldridge said. 'I'm that tired I couldn't get into a bath of water.'

They were referring to the second of his exploits in the district. The first had been to roam the town fighting drunk one night, shooting the bottles off the shelves in a succession of bars. An indulgent commanding officer had redeemed him from the clutches of the Military Police and let him off with a few days' field punishment. The second had been to announce, on the crowded staircase of a brothel, that he would set up an attendance record in a period of seven days, if other people would provide the money, at five shillings a time. He had found enough backers to set up an impressive score—I forget now what it was: I only remember how ugly it was to see the men who hated him egging him on—and at the end of the week he had challenged us to ask the girls at the brothel if we didn't believe him.

He pulled a chair from another table and sat down next to the girl. 'What's your name, chick?'

'Régine.'

He put his hand on her knee. 'You like jig-a-jig?'

She sat still and indifferent. Trower rose, took Eldridge by the arm and said, 'Come over to the bar and I'll buy you a drink.'

'What's wrong with here?'

'You heard the offer.'

Eldridge rose. 'I never say no.' He bent down and kissed Régine lightly on the cheek. 'I'll see you again, chick. When I'm in the mood.' He followed Trower to the bar. I watched him with hatred and with envy of his confidence. Régine sat and dreamed with a veiled, haughty expression.

I said, hoping to please her, '*Canaille.*' She made an indifferent pout, dismissing him from our conversation, and said, 'A soldier.'

She said that she had not seen me here before, and I replied that it was my first visit. I asked her if she played here every night, and she answered that she did. We ran out of conversation. I wanted to assail her more directly; but from the moment that Eldridge had touched her cheek she had remained as still as a statue. In the motionless, lifted poise of her head and the emptiness of her look I imagined disgust, weariness at the males who came, one after another, to sniff at her like dogs. I was afraid that if I moved closer the same disgust would roll out over me. I said, 'What time do you finish here each night?'

'I can go now if I want to.'

'Why don't you? You look so tired. Where do you live?'

'At the Hotel des Palmiers. It's not far, just at the other end of this street.'

'Come on, then. Let me see you home.'

'As you wish.'

We left, and walked down the dark, cobbled street together. I held her arm as gently as I could. The doorway of the Hotel des Palmiers was a dark slot between two shops. We paused outside. I said, 'I don't know when I shall be in town again. But I shall come to the bar again to see you. Do you mind?'

I thought she was going to say something. There was a fleeting dilation of the eyes, and a second's inquiring scrutiny. Then, in a voice that suddenly seemed crushed with fatigue, she said, 'As you wish.'

I did not kiss her; I was still thinking of Eldridge; but I returned to the billets feeling confused and happy.

I was not able to get into Ostend during the following few weeks. We had moved into a little seaside resort which the Germans had recently abandoned. The rows of empty villas, with their shutters closed and their stucco walls discoloured by the incessant rain, looked pathetic against their vast background of sea and cloud. They were extensively booby-trapped, and sappers were searching through them, helped by men from other units who, like myself, had been trained in the work.

I enjoyed this job. It engaged the mind and played upon the nerves without overstraining them, a puzzle game with a lethal forfeit involved. I was given the two best men in the company to help me: Trower and—I had to swallow my dislike, for he was not only fearless but quick to learn—Eldridge.

I thought a lot about Régine. Sometimes I let myself daydream, imagining stories in which we settled down together and warmed the bitterness out of each other's bones. It was the first time for some years that I had taken a girl seriously, thinking in terms of a future. I looked forward with a vague, tender pleasure to our next meeting, and did not talk to anyone about her.

In this rosy state, I began to get on well with Eldridge. At night, when the rest of us huddled by candlelight in the bare rooms of our billets, stirring only to prowl out into the cold for firewood, Eldridge would disappear, trekking off mysteriously into the darkness and coming back at dawn, sometimes drunk but always in time for his duties, and usually with a bottle of cognac to keep us warm. We were grateful, and not over-curious about his trips. Regulations that confined us to our quarters meant nothing to him. He probably had a whole network of arrangements with army drivers that enabled him to go back and forth to the towns along the coast. In silent streets, behind the shuttered doors of inconspicuous houses, a whole world of illicit occupations flourished: brothels, drinking-dens, black-market restaurants, gambling houses, lodgings for deserters. It was possible—for in the days that followed there was an increase in Eldridge's prosperity that he did not try to conceal, displaying a well-filled wallet, gambling lavishly, buying himself a circle of toadies—that he had joined one of the many gangs of soldiers who plundered army stores for the black market. After all, he was a good soldier of the old school. However, we drank his cognac, glowed with warmth and felt some kindness for him.

At length Trower and I got another pass to Ostend. At seven o'clock in the evening we went to the dancing-bar. Régine was not there. It was maddening to wait in the thick, smoke-hung warmth, with girls brushing invitingly past every moment, amid the clatter of plates and the ceaseless braying of the band. Trower gave up trying to keep me talking; he sat back in his chair and watched me silently.

At a few minutes before eight, the door opened. For the hundredth time I awoke with expectation. She entered. I was half out of my chair when I sat down again. Trower said, 'Don't look so tragic. Finish your drink.'

She was with Eldridge. She walked across the room with her arm through his, clasping herself raptly to his side. In the crowd, she seemed to stand apart; her body seemed to be making a proclamation; her step was happy, her cheeks had assumed a full, catlike shape of contentment. I sat there humiliated by the transformation in her, by my own failure to understand her, by the memory of my vague dreams, by the fact that the man was Eldridge. How could she? How *could* she?

Trower smiled ironically, without any sign of pity. 'Want to go?'

I watched them sitting at a table across the room, and answered with craven heartiness, 'No, don't be a fool'

'Want to dance? There's a nice little blonde over there giving you the eye.'

'You dance.'

He called a waiter, ordered two brandies, said to me, 'They're both for you,' and went across to the blonde.

Eldridge and Régine rose from their table and joined in the dance. As they moved about the floor she almost lay upon him. She appeared unaware of anything outside his sheltering arms.

Their dance brought them close to my table. Eldridge saw me. Beaming with friendship, he led Régine towards me, saying, 'Howdo, corporal.' She greeted me with a passing glance of bare recognition, and stood by his side holding his hand. 'Well,' Eldridge said, 'I won't wait for an invite this time.' He sat down, and Régine quietly seated herself at his side.

'I'll get you a drink,' he said.

'I've got these.'

'Ah, come on, I'll get you a bottle. Champagne.' He beamed again. 'A pal's a pal, eh, boy? Ah, there's your mate.' Trower had come back to the table.

I said, 'He wants to buy us champagne.'

Trower sat down. 'I wondered where the money was coming from.'

The remark mystified me. Eldridge uttered a happy hoot of laughter. 'Aye, I'm on to a cushy thing here.' He laid a hand on the girl's shoulder.

'She's a good little worker, this one.' He shook his head appreciatively. 'It's a funny life this. A bloody homeless dog one week and live like a prince the next. Waiter!'

Trower said, 'Don't trouble. We're drinking brandy. And we're not short.'

'Ah, you're slow, boy. Never refuse a drink. What's up with your mate here? He's looking blue.' He turned to me. 'Here, you want warming up, boy. Is it the judy?'

'Forget it.'

'You had a fancy for her, didn't you, boy?' His voice was full of a näive solicitude. 'Here, cheer up, boy. You can have her.'

Trower said, 'Take her away and drown her.'

'Ah, you leave the boy alone. He's sweet on her. A'n't you, boy? Go on, take her down the road. Two hundred francs for anyone else. Nowt for you. I tell you, a pal's a pal.'

I was paralysed with misery. It was like a bad dream. My ears rang with disbelief. I sat there and looked at her.

I was foolish enough to expect some kind of acknowledgement in her glance; shame, perhaps, or defiance, or self-justification, or even accusation, for I knew now what had really happened between us at the door of the Hotel des Palmiers. Her eyes rested on me, careless, disdainful.

'She's a fierce little armful, boy,' he said. 'The best I've had for a long time. I've recommended her to a few this last week or two, and I've had no complaints. Go on, boy, it's only just down the road. She's got a nice little room. Take as long as you like. Only bring her back when you've finished. Don't do to spoil 'em, eh?'

I was thinking of the money I had seen in his wallet, and his nightly disappearances, of the cognac he had given us. The terrible thing was that he was so hearty, so friendly, so unmalicious. It was beyond him to imagine a woman being more to anyone than the tamed animal that she was to him. Nothing that he did to her could weigh upon his conscience. He probably thought of himself as her benefactor. And to me he was being, according to his lights, a good friend.

'Go on, boy. She likes you. She don't mind obliging. Eh, chick? Jig-a-jig with corporal?'

The last few words were the first in the conversation which she had been able to understand. She said, in a bored voice, 'If he wishes.' Her attention was straying, her foot tapping wishfully to the rhythm of the dance.

I said to Trower, 'We'll go if you're ready.'

He answered brutally, 'Finish your drinks.' To Eldridge he said, in a flat voice, 'Have much trouble with her?'

'Nah. I know 'em. A couple of nights with her, she was clinging on to me like the ivy to the old oak tree. She couldn't do without me. That's when you've got 'em where you want 'em.' He chuckled in happy reminiscence. 'The third night I told her to get up and get weaving. She didn't savvy. I said, "Jig-a-jig, chick. Soldiers. Beaucoup francs for nous." She sat there and sulked for a bit. She sits there for about five minutes. She don't say a word. I let her brood. I know 'em, boy. Then she shrugs her shoulders, and she gets up, and she says, "Allons." So there you are, boy—' He was talking to me again. He was earnest, fatherly. It was monstrous. '—you've got to be firm with 'em. Let 'em know they need you. They'll crawl, boy. They'll never let you go.'

Trower said to him, 'I hope she's grateful.'

'Ah, she loves me.' Eldridge squeezed her arm indulgently. 'Don't you, chick?' She came to life with a pleased little smile. There was nothing demonstrative in her attitude now. What I saw was even more painful: the matter-of-fact security, the complacent response of a young wife. I felt the flow of shared secrets between them. He said, 'She's a lucky girl. I'm the one to look after her. Eh, chick?' He squeezed her arm again. She took his hand and held it tightly in hers, as if for reassurance.

Trower said, 'She wants to dance.'

Eldridge chuckled. 'You're right, Trower. You're another chap as knows the women. Come on, love.' They rose. 'Don't go away, lads. We'll be back.'

'Do us a favour and die first.' Trower's voice remained conversational.

'Eh?' Eldridge laughed, unoffended. 'What's up with you?'

'You spoil the view.'

'—you, brother. I'm too bad to die. Old Nick couldn't stand the competition.'

Trower said, 'Ah.' As the two of them drifted away into the dance, he followed them with his black, deliberate stare.

I said, 'For God's sake, let's beat it.'

He rose and stood over me. He said coldly, 'You had your chance.'

We left in silence. A few yards down the street he took my arm and bundled me into another bar. He ordered brandies and pushed a glass towards me. When I had drunk it he gave me another, and then another, until I was hot and stupid. There was a truck to carry us back to the billets, and he took me to it. Neither of us spoke another word that night—not even a 'goodnight' when we went to bed.

The Venus Bar

W hen Frank Chase asked us, 'Do you want to see a beautiful woman?' we stopped and took notice.

Frank was different from the rest of us. He kept to himself a good deal, not out of surliness but because he was given to meditation. There was a tranquil, reflective air that never left him, even in times of haste and danger. However sociable he might be, he always seemed to have one ear cocked to listen to some private debate that was going on inside him. He read a lot—religion, politics, philosophy—and although I was reading more at that time than I ever had before, I was not yet able to cope with the kind of books that absorbed him. I had become friendly with him in Sicily, and since Normandy he had been my lance-corporal. He had been a good colleague in everything connected with soldiering, but I was particularly glad because he was the first acquaintance I had ever had with whom I could thrash out ideas at all deeply. It was in this, I think, that I saw more clearly the difference between him and the rest of us. Most of us were, although not fundamentally unwilling, conscripts in the spirit as well as the flesh. Frank was in the war with his whole heart. For him, ideas were a starting-point; for us, an afterthought. A schoolmaster, twenty-nine years old and senior to most of us, his whole inner life was given to working out a vision of the world. The war, to him, was the fiery enactment of that vision. Our weary trudge was his crusade. And this, as will appear later, lends a particular significance to the adventure in which he became involved.

Naturally, his experience of women, and his attitude to them, differed from ours. He had behind him a youth in which sexual relationships had not been merely a means of elementary companionship and perhaps physical relief, but a school of social and intellectual development, equipping its graduates to understand the broader pattern of life. It was not surprising, then, that he was more fastidious than us.

From time to time one of us would point out a girl to him and say, 'Isn't she lovely?' or 'There's a beauty for you!' or 'What do you think of this one?'

He would smile tolerantly at the girl in question, dumpy little Sicilian or red-armed Flemish wench, and repeat the promise he had so often made to us, 'One day I'll show you what a beautiful woman really looks like.'

Now he was offering to show us. It was quite an occasion.

We were in Ostend, free for three days, with our pockets full of pay, and his gesture had brought us to a stop outside the big plate-glass window of the Venus Bar.

Another man's idea of a beautiful woman is always liable to come as a shock. Frank's confident gesture had staggered us. It was not merely that the woman appeared ugly to us; she was of an appearance that aroused an animal hostility in us. I felt as if I were looking at a snake. Alone in the bar, apart from the waiter and barman in a shadowy background, she sat at a table near the window, aware of our stare but looking indifferently beyond us. She was small, with a slim, supple-looking body. She had a small head, with black hair that shone flat against her skull. It was the shape of her head, as well as the cruel, direct gaze of her eyes, small, with blue shadows painted beneath them, and the sleek tightness with which her lovely skin was drawn over the narrow cheekbones; it was this, and her poise, upright, graceful and menacingly still, that reminded me of a snake's head lifted up to strike.

She was beautifully dressed. I cannot remember how, at this distance of time, but I have an impression of a black costume, moulded to a bosom that was surprisingly full for that lithe body, and flaring out to spread about the ankles; a white pearl choker showing off both her slender neck and the black silk that clad her shoulders; and a small toque-like hat fitting upon the back of the head. Her poise, sitting at the table, was relaxed but full of authority. She must have embodied for Frank, with her clothes and her clever, perfect face, a whole world of civilisation; and ignoring him, she held him there, brooding and glowing, while the rest of us exchanged glances.

He said, 'I'm going in. No need for you chaps to come.' He indicated the wooden OUT OF BOUNDS signboard nailed over the doorway by the Military Police. 'I'll see you back at the hotel.'

We had no wish to accompany him, and still less to burden him with our presence. We walked away, and did not see him for another three days. What happened to him in that time I heard from him later.

He entered, said, '*Bonjour*, mademoiselle,' to the woman and sat at another table. He ordered a drink and told the waiter to ask the lady if she would give him the pleasure of permitting him to order something for her. The waiter went across to the woman and spoke to her.

She glanced across at Chase and said to him in French—she had heard him speaking to the waiter in that language—'If you want a girl the waiter will get you one.'

He answered, 'I'm sorry you've misunderstood me, mademoiselle. If I hoped for anything, it was for your advice. I have three days to spend here, and I would be grateful for some information about the town.'

Her voice remained cold. 'The waiter is a well-informed man.'

Chase said that he was sure of it, and a short silence followed, during which the woman continued looking out of the window. Then she said, in a hard voice, 'You know this place is out of bounds to soldiers?'

'I can understand why, when a small glass of beer costs forty francs.' (This was four shillings in English money.)

'Why do you come here, then?'

'Why do you come here, mademoiselle?'

'I am the owner.'

He begged her pardon.

She repeated, 'Why do you come here when my bar is out of bounds?'

He replied with some nonsense about the charm of the forbidden.

'That may be,' she said, 'but it would be better if you left. I obey the authorities in all respects.'

Chase rose, and made a little bow of acquiescence.

She smiled, ironically, and said, 'An unusual NCO, I must say. And you speak French well, monsieur. Do you speak any other languages?'

'Some German.'

She took him up in perfect German. 'I don't doubt it. After all, your job requires it, doesn't it?'

Her words, and the tone of her voice, puzzled him. 'What job?'

Her elbows on the table, she rested her chin on her hands and pondered for a few moments, the dark, contracting pupils of her eyes unwaveringly upon him. 'No, I think, after all, you're not—'

He walked across to her table and asked her to enlighten him.

'—You're not from the Field Security Police.'

He burst out laughing at the idea. 'I'm flattered. But why are you so sure I'm not a police spy? I can understand your suspicion in the first place.'

'You were with those other men, who are at the Hotel Excelsior, marching soldiers, soldiers on leave. I know about them, I know they are genuine. You are an educated man, but you have hands like a labourer's—scars, callouses, hard yellow skin that will never come clean, a black dead nail. It takes a long time to get hands like that, a long time of hardship, with those other soldiers. Your cheeks are hollow and there's no blood in your lips. You have been wet and freezing and tired, and that shows for a long time after. It is plain where you have been, and policemen don't come from there. Besides'—once more she permitted herself to smile—'the police smell is lacking. And that is something about which I have an instinct. Come and sit with me. Not here, but in the alcove, where you can't be seen from the street.'

In the alcove, where they were hidden from the view of any passing police patrol, she called the waiter. He bobbed a bow, 'Madame Magda desires—?'

She ordered brandies.

Chase, sitting back with both hands on the table, echoed the name as he studied her. 'Magda.' She looked at him questioningly. He said, 'Why should you fear the Field Security Police?'

'I don't fear them. But it is my habit to be careful. They are prejudiced against me.'

'Is that why they put your place out of bounds?'

'Perhaps. They didn't tell me.'

'Why are they prejudiced against you?'

'Because the Gestapo didn't close me down. Isn't that ridiculous?'

'You were open when the Germans were here?'

'Naturally.'

'And why did the Gestapo leave you alone?'

'Because I paid them well for it. I expect I shall soon be paying your police well, too.'

'Was there any reason why they might not have left you alone?'

'I am Polish.' She cut his next question short. 'Never mind my life story. Tell me, you are an educated man. Why are you only a common soldier?'

'I am happy as I am. My ambitions are not military.'

'What are they, then?'

'Literary.'

'Ah!' Chin in cupped hand, she looked at him with an understanding that was strangely childlike in her worldly face. 'That explains you. Scholars are not practical people. Otherwise you would have looked after yourself better. I knew a Doctor of Philosophy once. In Hamburg. What a donkey!'—she trailed off into a few seconds of silent reminiscence. '—People like you need looking after. You could do better for yourself.'

'For example?'

'Clever men stay warm and safe. In the army or out of it. There are plenty of fools to march and freeze and die in the fields. For a man with brains there is always something better.' She fell silent again, facing him across the table with her cold, level look. 'I am glad my conversation is interesting to you. You are interesting to me, too. I hope you will stay and dine with me.'

'Thank you, Magda. I accept with pleasure.'

They talked non-committally until it was time to leave. They both told the sort of stories that strangers in bars in wartime tell each other. She talked in an intimate, professionally knowing way, about the girls who frequented the bar, their personal oddities, the foibles of male behaviour that they came across, the funny or ironic adventures in which they became involved. He had his own fund of encounters and experiences to relate, grim, comical, bitter, ridiculous.

They walked through the dark, cobbled streets and stopped outside a shuttered house. Magda knocked. The door was opened slightly, she was inspected and they were admitted.

A dark hall and another doorway led to the restaurant. Chase, who had spent the past weeks trudging in the mud and huddling in cold, lamplit cellars, eating his meals cold, perhaps in drizzling rain, out of a mess-tin, must have wondered if he was dreaming of some forbidden paradise. Forbidden it certainly was, for in that time of severe rationing places like this were outside the law, hidden from the knowledge of hungry human kind. The room was warm, lit only by small, scallop-shaded lamps on the tables and in the corners. The walls were panelled with cream and pink silk, in quilted patterns. A waiter led them to a table which, like the other small tables dotted about the room, was covered with a spotless tablecloth of white damask that hung in thick folds almost to the floor, and with dazzling cutlery. In the centre of the table was a basket of fruit—incredible to his eyes in this desolate land, and at that wintry season—heaped with black grapes, ripe, satiny peaches and big, juicy pears. Among the people who sat at the other tables were a few British officers, mostly of senior rank, who glanced at Chase curiously but did not interfere with him. There were many of the smart, hard, mercenary girls he had seen in the more expensive bars; and there were men in civilian clothes who were of two kinds. Some of them were middle-aged, big and prosperous men, who entered in heavy but beautifully cut overcoats, whose faces, as they moved from the shadows into the soft circles of light around their tables, were sleek and strong, and whose soft controlled voices, as they bowed with an air of mocking courtesy to their women, were full of shrewdness, sensuality and cynicism. They were men who seemed to be pricing everything and everyone they looked at; and the even murmur of their conversation always had the sound of business about it. The rest were young men, with firm, sharply profiled faces and alert, watching eyes, most of whom were loudly dressed and all of whom seemed to be sitting in a kind of tigerish silence while their girls chattered to them.

It was a strange contrast, all this, to the world outside, where the shawled women queued for hours, in icy rain, for bread and where, a few miles farther away, the soldiers crept along the dykes like sodden rats under the same wet freezing lash.

When Chase told us about the meal that was served to him, we did not believe him; or at least, we thought he was indulging in the pardonable exaggeration of the storyteller. It was not until after the war, when I was entertained in Paris, that I realised that such meals could be had on this earth. First the waiter brought a whole lobster on a silver tray. Frank and Magda heaped their plates with round, juicy slices from the body and went on to open the bright red claws with silver nutcrackers. Then came beautiful little spring chickens, roasted all crisp and golden in delicious gravy. Plates of artichokes followed. Then huge, tender steaks. A little later the waiter came with cheeses on a trolley. Frank thought that this was the end of the meal, but Magda explained that the cheese was to cleanse his mouth of the taste of the meat, before the dessert was served. There were two dessert courses; first a pudding of thick cream full of liqueur and preserved fruits, with which a champagne was served; and then pancakes covered with burning rum. Apart from the champagne, four wines were served with the meal—there was even a separate wine for the cheese—and afterwards there was coffee and old brandy.

'I loved it,' Chase told me. And it seemed to me that there was guilt in his voice as he made this admission. For he was the slave of his conscience, and examined the right and wrong of everything he did in the light of his ideals. When there was room for two men in a warm nook and the rest had to sleep in the wet, Frank thought it a crime to be one of the two. We others were against the black market, but we would never reject a gift that came from it. Frank, ordinarily, would not eat a mouthful of food that was not rightfully his. But that night, wine, and brandy, and food, and the dreamlike suddenness with which he had been wafted out of our life of wretchedness, had lulled him.

After dinner, while he was smoking a cigarette, Magda said to him, 'Do you know, there are deserters in this room? British deserters, and German deserters, too?'

Chase replied that he did not doubt it. He was in a complacent stupor. It seemed natural to him, in that condition, that the faces of the young men—which were like so many of the faces he had seen under the rims of British and German steel helmets—were the faces of deserters. And above all, at that time, it seemed natural to come across deserters. As the dreary winter advanced, the armies on both sides were crumbling at the edges, and the number of deserters—eighteen thousand, it was rumoured, from the British front alone—was one of the great topics of discussion among the soldiers. It was a common occurrence, in canteens and restaurants behind the lines, for the orchestra suddenly to stop playing and the raiding group of Military Police, moving in from guarded doorways, to inspect the documents of the men who sat silently at their tables. Most men did not desert because it did not occur to them, and because the only human oasis in a fearful world seemed to be with the comrades they knew. But at this time, when the low, leaden skies reflected the universal spirit, when the last sparks of enthusiasm died under the endless, penetrating rain, and when the long-concealed blunders and quarrels of generals had at last become common knowledge in the ranks, the hope of ever finishing the war had faded out and a nightmarish sense of perpetual imprisonment spread like an infection. Was this the mysterious 'deserter-land' into which thousands had vanished? Frank Chase, half-asleep over his cigarette, heard himself answer, 'Good luck to them.'

He went home with Magda. Her flat was lavishly but, to his mind, vulgarly furnished. How serpentine, cunning and subtly muscular a slim little female body could be, he learned for the first time; but, looking down afterwards at her sleeping face, it occurred to him that not once in that night had a flicker of genuine feeling disturbed its cruel calm.

They slept late the next morning, and a middle-aged housekeeper brought their lunch to them in bed. In the morning, Magda's manner towards him was more relaxed than it had been. She no longer spoke to him and watched him in the same controlled, cat-and-mousehole way as on the previous evening. She walked about the room, talking in a higher, clearer voice than before, the words coming more rapidly, her guard dropped. Like a wife, she talked when she had her back to him, not ceasing when she was letting a garment fall over her head. She told him how they were to spend the day with the sharp, clear confidence of one giving orders without fear of demur; and she spoke, now, about herself.

She had been born in a criminal quarter of Warsaw. Calmly, while she was combing her hair, she told him of the warren of slums in which she had grown up, where the crimes of elders were commonplaces of childish conversation, murder a badge of pride, jail sentences part of the normal pattern of life. The thin, dirty little children, intently watching the swarming pageant of vice from dark corners, discussed with all the seriousness of play the methods and rewards of selling one's self, and when she was thirteen she followed the example of her older playmates by earning her first few shillings from a man.

At the age of fifteen she had been enlisted, with a group of other girls, by one of the agents who came from abroad to collect recruits from this teeming nursery of corruption. As eager as any young emigrant off to make a career for herself, she went with the party to Hamburg, where she was placed in a brothel in the waterfront district.

It was at this point of her narrative that the first trace of real feeling came into her voice, which rang with complacent pride as she described the next turn in her career. Her tender years, and the cunning air of frail dependence which she adopted as the basis of her technique, won her several admirers, particularly among the more prosperous clients whose thirst for new sensations brought them to this low-class house. The Doctor of Philosophy had been among them. Another had been a business man, the agent of a Solingen steel firm who regularly visited Hamburg on business.

The only bonds that kept her in Hamburg were debt and the vigilance of her bully—a young man she had been forced to accept as a protector against all the other birds of prey who threatened girls like her—and one night, with the help of the man from Solingen, she ran away. For a year, living in Solingen in a room that the business man had provided for her, she plundered him of money and gifts, and although she had promised him to give up prostitution, she took advantage of his frequent absences to ply her trade industriously and lucratively.

Her greatest advantage, she told Chase with satisfaction, was that she was never in danger of falling for a man—unlike most of the girls she knew, who were always flinging themselves and all their earnings at the feet of some man or other. She was full of contempt for all the wretched little creatures who could still, after all their experience with men, fall in and out of love. She had no gifts to spare for any other member of the human race, and her own flesh was no more than her first piece of working capital, which would enable her to multiply her assets. At the end of a year, with a substantial amount saved, she left Solingen and established herself in Berlin.

'It's a business,' she said. 'You have to look at everything like a business. That's the main thing.' She used her savings as an investment, spending them on good clothes and a smart flat, and establishing herself as a high-class practitioner of her profession. Her status enabled her to be selective. She concentrated on business men, and by nineteen thirty-three, with the help of some of her clients, who provided loans, advice and in one or two cases investments, she was the proprietress of a night club. 'With girls, of course,' she said. 'I was twenty-three years old. It was an achievement, don't you think?'

The Nazis came to power in the same year and Magda, as a foreigner, was in a delicate position. For three years she carried on in Berlin, keeping in the good books of police, Gestapo and Party officials with bribes and lavish entertainments.

In nineteen thirty-six, guided by the instincts with which people like her are endowed, she decided that it was time to leave Germany. She sold her interests, bought jewellery, bribed frontier officials, and arrived in Belgium with a small fortune in her week-end case. Within four years, she was the owner of three well-appointed bars, in Brussels, Ostend and Antwerp. 'And of course, girls at all of them. Girls of the highest class, each one chosen by me.'

The war came, and in nineteen-forty the German occupation. 'I decided,' she explained seriously, 'to establish myself in Ostend. Antwerp is a dock town—there might have been air-raids. Brussels was too near the centre of things. Too many Gestapo, too many people to bribe, and perhaps some who could not be bribed. Ostend was quiet, it seemed reasonably safe, you can always come to terms with the authorities in a small place—and business was likely to be good, with so many German officers here.'

Within a year or two she was at the height of her career. She was spending more in bribes alone than she had ever earned before—as a Pole, a member of an 'inferior' people, she was eligible for forced labour—but with business booming, she hardly noticed the expense.

'There was a big Luftwaffe establishment here. I had everything in my pocket. I supplied the officers' mess with everything—wines, meat, tinned foods, lingerie to send home, girls. They were always satisfied with the girls I sent them. I lived in this town like a queen. I was on the most intimate terms with the commanding officer of the depot—and that paid, I can assure you. It was the best protection.'

She was sitting at a dressing-table, fastening a bracelet on her wrist. He was behind her, and she spoke to his image in the mirror. 'Well, you know how it is in business. The bottom always drops out of a boom.' She shrugged her shoulders. 'You have to expect it, and there's no point in mourning over it. The British arrived, and my business vanished overnight. I lost a lot over that "liberation", believe me. Still, if you have a good head, there is always something. After all, what's the difference between British officers and German officers? I'm building the business up again already.'

She rose to her feet and stood, sleek and beautified, at the foot of the bed on which he sprawled. 'Thank God there's still a shortage of everything. Now that your people are bringing in supplies, I can get all the goods I want. I'm making contacts every day at your dumps. Bread, meat, blankets, medical supplies, clothing, petrol, automobile parts. The market is wonderful. Everything's gold these days. And now at last your people have captured Antwerp—it was intolerable, the time they took over it—I can deal there. That's where the real money is, in Antwerp. So you can see for yourself there's a future in my business. You've not been very clever in the past, for a man of learning, but you may find that getting to know me is the cleverest thing you've ever done. Come!' She held out her hand. 'Let's go down to the bar. They get slack if I don't shake them up every day.'

They went down to the Venus Bar. In the evening they went dancing, then to the restaurant for another sumptuous dinner. After that, a second night of Magda's cold, accomplished lust.

The next afternoon they made their daily call at the bar. Rain was falling, not the sleety drizzle of the preceding days, but a battering, continuous downpour. Frank and Magda sat in the alcove, watching the street. Soldiers were marching past—reinforcement drafts, probably, being hurried from the docks to the transit camp where they would wait till the hungry front line cried out for its next human meal. Every few minutes another little phalanx came marching down the cobbled street. The soldiers moved calf-deep through a blur of bouncing raindrops, whose hiss mingled with the quick crash of their boots and the splash of water they threw up. The men were as bulky as cattle with their green, gleaming-wet gas capes spread over the burden of their packs and weapons. Stooping under the weight of their gear, packed in a close, surging huddle, with lowered heads, they poured through the narrow street like steers into a casting-pen. The rain rattled on their steel helmets and streamed off their capes. Their swift and regular movement continued past the window, as relentless as the movement of time, the crash of their boots setting up a rhythm not gay in its brisk tempo but heartbreaking, a quick drum-crash that was hastening them out of the living world.

'Well,' Magda said, with her cold smile. 'You're better off in here than out there.'

'I'm going back out there today. My leave ends tonight.'

'You're really going back?'

He was only listening idly, and he answered idly, 'What else?'

Magda laughed. 'They always told me that the English were slow-witted.'

Her tone caught his attention. 'Why?'

'What do you think I've been trying to show you these last three days?'

'You've been very kind.'

'Kind!' She uttered a sound of scorn. 'You don't think I'm a Sister of Charity, do you? You've been living in the world of fools.' She indicated the marching men. 'Their world. It suited me to show you the world of people with brains. Why? Why did I tell you about my business, and my plans? Didn't you think?'

'Yes,' he answered slowly. 'I thought. Go on.'

'Listen!' She leaned across the table and clasped the back of his wrist with a cold, firm little hand. 'I need a man like you. I already have soldiers working for me, but they are half-wits—sneak-thieves or fat officers on the make. I want someone like you to help me deal with them. You're educated, you can speak three languages, you know the regulations of the Army and how it's organised. There's so much that you can do. I want someone who can get into the dumps for me, find what they have and who is willing to get stuff out. I want someone who can go into the cafés and the canteens, and find the right men, and bring them to me. I want to be able to send an Army lorry to Brussels or Antwerp or Ghent, and know that the man I send with it can wear a British uniform and bluff his way past any police patrol that stops him. I want him to be able to dress as an officer or an ordinary soldier, as the need arises. You will have all the clothes and documents you require to keep you safe. In civilian clothes, talking French, with the right papers in your pocket, the Army will never catch you. When you are in uniform the Belgian authorities will never challenge you. It's perfect. You'd be safe, and you'd be rich. Forget about going back. Stay and work for me.'

His silence encouraged her. 'You ought to be proud I picked you up,' she urged. 'A self-made woman like me! I've paid you a compliment. Don't you think I count as much as anyone in these parts?—Mijnheer van This, with his fishing fleet, or Burgemeester That, with his factory? For all their graces I'm as smart as they are. That's the life you want to get into, my friend, where all the little vermin rushing at each other in their field-grey and their khaki don't mean a thing to you.'

The soldiers marched past. The rain rushed and splashed and pelted down, forcing them to lower the dead grey lumps that they wore for faces.

'I'll pay you ten thousand francs a week—what's that, fifty pounds, isn't it, in your money? And a percentage on every deal. I'll find you a beautiful flat. If it's girls you want, I have the best on the coast. I'm offering you the biggest chance of your life.'

Without looking at her, he shook his head.

'You're not afraid, are you?'

'No, I'm not afraid.'

She resumed her arguments, the harsh vibration of contempt steadily growing in her voice. He was not listening. What crushed him, he told me later, in those moments after his refusal, was the realisation that he had hesitated. He had hesitated for a few seconds before shaking his head; and all at once he had taken the measure of his own weariness.

In that moment, it had not been his ideals which came into his mind, but a calculation, the same calculation that any exhausted, tempted soldier might have made: the moment you desert, she'll have you at her mercy. Never mind her documents, never mind her ten thousand francs, never mind her percentages. You'll be in her hands every second of your life. She can pay you or not, as she likes, and she can make you do what she likes. The moment you step out of line, or the moment she has no more use for you, she can give you to the police with a snap of her fingers.

Then the moment had flashed past, and all the reasons of conscience had come marching into his mind like a Salvation Army band. For another man the refusal would have been sufficient. Memory would have censored the moment of hesitation and lingered complacently over the virtuous reasons, the manly decision. Not so with Frank Chase. For him the moment was irrevocable, its scar of self-reproach permanent.

Where was his former purity of belief, that he had remained for these three days, stunned by pleasure, in the company of all that he hated? A year ago—he remembered all he had said to his friends about having no traffic with evil—he would not even have consented to speak with this woman. Under the pressures and changing temperatures of war the human spirit undergoes molecular changes as inevitable as those that occur in metals under stress. He had looked upon himself, strengthened by his intellect, as immune from those changes, which he had seen in others around him. Now he knew that he, too, had changed, and that however firm he might remain on the surface, in the spirit he was at one with the most reluctant and weary of his fellow-soldiers, with the apathetic German prisoners he had so often escorted, at one, indeed, with the swarming deserters he had once condemned.

He dreaded to go back to his unit now, for every burden would henceforward be harder to bear than before, every freezing pellet of rain would seem like a last unendurable stroke. And for how long more? For him, too, the war had now become eternity.

Magda had finished speaking and was waiting, her face nakedly vicious.

He said, 'Don't waste your breath, Magda. I'm quite satisfied to go on being a fool.'

Another squad of soldiers went by, with a steady, miserable splashing of boots in puddles.

'And why?'

'Because—' And here, if he had been less of a Puritan, he might have realised that the weakness he had in common with his fellows was not a flaw, but his own most precious humanity; that what mattered in him was not the change, the cowardly calculation, but the ability he shared with his comrades to keep the contract of faith. But he would never give himself any credit. He was doomed, being what he was, to punish himself. '—I don't know why I waste time telling you, Magda. The language is one you'll never understand. But I pray for the fools to inherit the earth.'

'Go on,' she said. 'Go on back to them, and freeze, and die of pneumonia.'

He walked to the door and paused for a moment, with his hand on the bar, while the rain hammered for him on the glass and another bowed, huddled mass of men trudged past.

'Go on,' she jeered. 'Clear out, go on after them!'

He opened the door and went out, after them, stooping as the rain laid its lash across his back.

Efficiency

January, nineteen forty-five: the scene, a beerhouse in Antwerp.

Five British soldiers are sitting round a table listening to Lieutenant Donovan, United States Engineers.

Lieutenant Donovan is a short, square man, good-looking, his black hair thick and glossy with life, his appearance and his movements giving the impression of a considerable inner force. The only officer in the party, he is friendly without being self-conscious. He is a little drunk, but the only sign of this is that his voice is unnaturally stern and solemn.

'I like you guys. Yeah, you Limeys are swell fellers, all of you. Dependable, that's what I like about you fellers. Say, in North Africa—any of you fellers in Africa? That was a dump. The Kasserine, that was the place. I sure won't forget the Kasserine in a hurry. You fellers sure helped us out of that one. It was the first time for us. The Krauts came in, we lit out like jack-rabbits. Yes, sir, I sure wouldn't like to write home about the Kasserine. Still, I guess there has to be a first time for everybody.

'But you know, the trouble with you guys, you're so slow. You're so God-damned slow. Say, listen. You guys been in this town long? You hear about the movie theatre? The movie theatre that was hit by a rocket? A few weeks back. I reckon the Krauts were lucky with that one. Right on the nose, bingo! There was a swell movie showing, too, Gary Cooper. Eight hundred people in the house, our Joes, your guys—y' know. Three o'clock in the afternoon. Wham, bang through the roof, this Heinie rocket bursts in the middle of them.

'Jesus, was that a mess! The roof and the walls came in. The place was just a heap. A couple of hundred guys came out, guys in the balconies, y' know. The others were underneath.

'So what happens? Your people move in to clear up. Feller in charge, Town Major I guess you call him, he goes along there with a bunch of your guys, and he starts clearing up. You shoulda seen the guy! Brick by brick, that was his way.

'Monday goes by, Tuesday, Wednesday. He's still clearing up. He's dug a coupla hundred stiffs out, the others are still underneath. Thursday. The Limeys are still carrying the bricks away. Thursday, the US Engineers move in. I come along, coupla trucks, work detail, all ready to go.

'"Listen, major," I say to this Limey. "I sure appreciate your thoroughness, but can't we speed the job up?" The major says, "I'd be delighted to, old boy, if you've any suggestions."

'"Sure I have," I say. "I'll get a coupla bulldozers. We'll rake this section flat in an afternoon."

'The major says, "But what about the dead?"

'"See here, major," I say, "They won't beef. Why should you?" He looks around sort of slow, and he says, sort of slow, "I'm sorry, old boy, but we've got to get them out."

'"I know what you're thinking, major," I tell him. "The US Army don't miss nothing. Those stiffs won't smell, don't worry. I've got that fixed. A coupla fire tenders with their tanks full of disinfectant. Hose the whole place over. We can shoot a ton of lime over it, too, if you want. Leave it to us."

'He shakes his head. "Sorry, lieutenant."

'I don't know what's eating the guy. I ask him, "Say, what is this, major? You figuring on making this a job for life?"

'He gives me another one of these slow looks, and he says, "Well, you see, we've got to give these poor chaps a Christian burial."

'Can you beat that? See here, fellers, I sure appreciate respect for the dead. I guess you fellers would think me crazy if I told you how much we spend back home on reverencing the dead. But you've got to be smart in this world. A war's a war. It's like business is business. You've got to have know-how, you've got to move fast, and you've got to get there ahead of the other guy.

'I try to tell him. He's very polite. He smiles. He nods his head. He says, "I admire you, lieutenant." And do you know what he says, with that slow sort of smile of his? "Some other time, perhaps, lieutenant."

'So what do I do? You can't argue with a nut like that. I pull my Joes out, and for all I know, your major is still in there, shifting that joint brick by brick.

'Like I say, you Limeys are good guys. I love you guys. I love all of you. But you've got to learn. You've got to be up to date. You just can't be choosy.

You can't *be* that way. Know-how. You can't get ahead in this man's world without know-how. And if you'll pardon my saying so, that's why we're going on up, and you're going on down.

'Another drink, fellers? Come on, let me get you another bottle. Say, you're not too proud to drink with an officer, are you? Let me tell you, it doesn't mean a thing to me. Not in my country, fellers. Ah, come on, you can't leave a guy on his own.'

Everybody Loves a Dog

A dog came loping into the bivouac area. He lifted his head and looked at the passing soldiers with liquid, imploring eyes. He nosed at the flaps of tents and made hungry mewing sounds. A soldier struck at him with a slat of wood and he scurried out of reach. He stood for a few moments, puzzled by his reception; then he came trotting back. Again he was driven out of the camp. He stood in the roadway, muzzle uplifted, trembling and apparently incredulous. He made a third attempt to enter the camp. This time the men stoned him. He bolted for a hundred yards, slowed down to a dejected, road-sniffing trot and vanished from sight.

A few years earlier, when the world had been a different place for us, we had behaved differently towards dogs. Encamped like holidaymakers in the calm countryside of England, we had adopted the dog as our sacred animal. Any dog was free to shelter in our huts, to sleep in our blankets, to feed from our mess-tins. We had found dogs, stolen dogs, kept them as mascots, smuggled them from camp to camp. But that had been four years earlier.

A new man came to us. He was a Yorkshireman. He was big, soft and stooping, his face pudgy and white, with small timid eyes and a voice almost too sullenly quiet to be audible. He trudged about the camp on his own, for he had come at a time when we no longer befriended newcomers, his collar turned up against the incessant thin rain, his hands in his pockets, the skirts of his greatcoat flapping about his legs.

On the third day with us he went for a walk and came back carrying the dog, a wet and shivering little creature, inside the breast of his greatcoat. He took it into his shelter, broke up some biscuits and shreds of beef, and fed it. The other men in the shelter watched him. One of them said, 'Get that pooch out of here.' The Yorkshireman answered in a low, dogged voice, 'It's doing no harm.'

'They got fleas.'

'They're as clean as you and me.'

MacAra—now a full corporal—picked up the dog, which let out a terrible yelp, and flung it through the doorway with all his force. Without a glance at anyone, the Yorkshireman turned up his collar and went out into the rain, slipping and stumbling on the muddy path.

He did not return till after dark. He lowered his head to enter the shelter, pulled off his sodden overcoat and crawled into his blankets. He lay with his back to the others, but pleasurable canine squeaks betrayed the presence of the dog in his bed. Man, dog and blanket were flung out into the mud.

He did not come back, and we found in the morning that he had moved into a ruined cottage. He slept on a stone floor that was wet and filthy. Rain dripped through the bare slats of the ceiling and was borne in through the gaping windows by each gust of cold wind that swept the room. Here he established his home, with the dog. The men jeered at him and called him Doggy. He did not answer, but walked about among us with a blank, lowered expression. There was no hope in his white, fat face. He could not understand how he had come into this world, where men plodded dully about as if it was natural to have rain everlastingly drizzling down and mud everlastingly underfoot, and where everyone seemed to take it for granted that a shelter made of shellboxes and tarpaulins was the highest attainable form of human habitation. We hated him because he had just come from Blighty, and this, too, he could not understand.

In the daytime, while he went about his duties, he left the dog tied up in the cottage, with plenty of food and water and a nest of sacking to sleep in. He dared not let the dog loose, for it would have come prowling into camp after him, to its peril. Once he muttered, 'It's a shame to tie a dog up.'

'I'm crying,' the corporal said.

'But he's only a pup. Don't you feel sorry for him?'

'Is anyone sorry for us?'

One day the order came to move. Sergeants lurched along the muddy paths calling their platoons together. Men packed their gear and broke down their shelters, folding tent cloths and tarpaulins and heaving them on to vehicles. For a couple of hours the camp swarmed with movement; then the men, bulky as bears in their greatcoats and packs, clustered round the lined-up lorries, and where the camp had been there was only a waste of grey mud, churned, rutted and littered with refuse.

The Yorkshireman appeared, burdened like everyone else, but looking even bulkier. He approached his officer and spoke to him. The officer said, 'Don't bother me, old chap, I'm busy,' and turned away.

He wandered off towards the other lorries, but Corporal MacAra called him back. 'You get on to that truck, and double quick.'

The Yorkshireman clambered up over the tailboard. A couple of other men seized hold of him and hauled him in to the truck, and he took his seat. Above his dirty ammunition pouches, between the constricting straps, his greatcoat bulged. He tried to hold the lapel down, but there was an excited heaving from beneath, glimpses of a black muzzle trying to thrust out, the shine of brown eyes and a breathless canine squealing.

The corporal said, 'I'm fed up with you.' He reached inside the man's coat, pulled the dog out and dropped it over the tailboard. The Yorkshireman did not resist, but sat slackly, looking at the floor.

The lorry began to move. It lurched through the mud, pulled out on to the road and took its place in the convoy as the next lorry, fifty yards behind, pulled out of the rank and followed. We sat along the sides of the lorry, looking out over the tailboard apathetically. Somebody said, 'Look, there's that bloody pup again.' The dog was chasing us, his legs trotting tirelessly under him. We watched idly, the Yorkshireman intently.

The lorry gathered speed. The dog scampered more rapidly, then lost hope and ran out to the roadside, where he stood and watched us speeding away.

The corporal leaned over the tailboard, whistled to the dog and made inviting gestures with his fingers. The Yorkshireman looked up at him in surprise. MacAra said, in a friendly voice, 'Go on, you whistle him. See if he comes.' The Yorkshireman's features expanded in bewildered relief, and he called the dog with a long, fluting whistle. The dog gathered itself up and shot down the road after us. The Yorkshireman cried, 'Theer he comes,' and he looked round at us, beaming. It was the first time we had seen him smile. The loneliness passed away across his face like the shadow of a cloud.

MacAra said to his lance-corporal, 'Fifty francs you can't hit him.'

The Yorkshireman must have only understood slowly. His smile persisted, then became fixed and silly. The lance-corporal dropped on one knee, raised his rifle, rammed the bolt home and, swaying with the lorry, took a shot at the scampering dog. The Yorkshireman seemed to deflate. He sagged back against the taut hood of the lorry, his head lolling to one side so that, still watching the dog, he appeared sightless. The only tension was in his hands, tightly gripping the barrel of the rifle that stood between his knees.

The dog had not noticed the shot, and was still bolting after the truck.

MacAra said, 'Call yourself a soldier?' He took the rifle, raised it, and fired from a standing position. The dog was lifted backward into the air, turned over in a somersault and hit the road. The driver of the truck behind us, keeping up the same steady speed as our own, raised his thumb to the corporal.

The corporal handed the rifle back to its owner. 'There,' he said. 'Fifty francs you owe me. Takes a soldier to do that.'

The Yorkshireman sat with his head bowed upon the muzzle of his rifle.

Victory Night

It's a good life,' Sergeant Craig said. 'You can't get away from the fact. If it wasn't for the wife and kiddy I think I'd sign up for the peacetime Army.' This statement, coming from a soldier in April, nineteen forty-five, was so startling that I might have challenged it if the sergeant had not changed the subject. 'Tell me, what do you think about Frank Chase?' His strong, youthful face, so smoothly gleaming that it showed hardly the shadow of a beard, was full of a naive concern.

'He's a good chap. What are you getting at?'

'I'm worried about him. He doesn't say a word when I talk to him. And I don't like that way he stares as if he can't see you. Corporal MacAra was telling me, he wakes up at nights sometimes, and however late it is, he always sees Chase wide awake, just sort of lying there, with a fag in his mouth and his hands under the back of his head, staring up at the ceiling.'

'Well, to be honest, I think he's ready for the boneyard.'

'That's what I was thinking.' I thought the sergeant was going to say more, but after a second's pause he walked away.

We were billeted in Holland at the time, in a state of restless, desolate idleness. It was clear that the war in Europe was coming to an end, petering out in a remote, nightmarish way that none of us had foreseen in our daydreams. It was fairly safe to assume that our own part in it was finished; but we were too tired and morose to feel aware of victory or even of reprieve.

A few of us were exempt from this state, and Sergeant Craig was one of them. This story is not about him, but it is necessary to say something of him at this point; because it is wrong to tell what happened to many, as these stories do, wrong to dwell on those who were brutalised or—as this story about Frank Chase will show—worn out by war, without remembering that there are people who can survive such experiences uncorrupted.

Yes, Sergeant Craig had changed since, in nineteen thirty-nine, he had reported to the depot as a twenty-one-year-old conscript. After all, he had been promoted, had married, fathered a child, been wounded twice and decorated with a Military Medal. His appearance was changed. He had filled out; the downy freshness in his cheeks was overlaid with a light, unblemished tan; and his bearing, once shy, was now authoritative. Inwardly, he had acquired confidence, decision and much practical wisdom. However, it was hard to see any other way in which he had changed.

He had not excessively aged, he had not become tired, callous, cynical or embittered. As a boy, he had left his job as a printer in a small Wiltshire town to answer the call of a loyalty which it was not in him to question, and after six years the same implicit loyalty sustained him. He was, I think, the only man in our circle who, after listening respectfully to a mutinous political discussion, could say, 'Well, I don't know, my King and Country are good enough for me,' with such simplicity that we in turn accepted his words with respect.

In battle he could be professionally calm and unmoved by suffering, but his ways of living had not coarsened. He was gay and boyishly flirtatious with women, but none of them tempted him to do anything more than show them his wife's photograph; and he gravely referred to them all, however sordid their backgrounds, as 'young ladies'. He did not use foul language, for he was too serene to need the relief it afforded, and too intelligent to require it as a reinforcement in his speech. He never wanted more to drink than a pint or two of cool beer.

He spoke to his men as if they were valued friends, always in the same quiet, respectful voice, and always showing an unsimulated interest in their various accomplishments and fields of knowledge; but he would allow them no familiarity towards him. They had to address him by his rank, never by his first name, and if any man lounged up to him, hands in pocket, the sergeant would daunt him into a more respectful posture with a level, questioning glance.

He was remorseless in forcing his men, as a group, to complete whatever task they had been given, but considerate in helping each individual along. He had eyes to see the weak but was deaf to the pleas of the malingerer. His bravery was inconspicuous. One only thought of it in retrospect. I always felt that, with him, courage was not fear overcome, but derived from the infinitude of his calm.

He took great care of his personal appearance, keeping his brass shining, his uniform carefully pressed, his belt and anklets spotlessly blancoed. The effect was not dandified but soldierly.

He liked soldiering. There was no neurotic longing for bloodshed in him. The battlefield was an ugly place to him, but it was the workshop in which a necessary job had to be done. And, although the job was unpleasant, he could not help finding it interesting. It is important to remember of men like Craig that it is not a cheap quickening of the blood that attracts them in war, but the finding of an object for their latent faculties, the development of skills, the testing of all the human virtues. He was not sickened and haunted by the sight of death and mutilation, for he was not afraid of these things himself, he was confident in his own capacities, and the gamble seemed to him a fair one for everyone to face. However, he was genuinely saddened to see men killed or wounded and indeed, because he alone had retained his innocence, he was the only one of us who did not affect callousness when talking of them. He could express grief simply and without shame, but he could shed memories before they lacerated him.

This was Sergeant Craig, then, his face shining with health and unmarked by strain in the midst of war-weariness and decay; a British soldier innocent and courageous, the unknowing continuer of a long tradition, resistant to the evils that had eaten into others because he was a simpler and sounder man. There are many like him, without whom any picture of our human kind is incomplete and false.

He came to me the next day. He said, 'Frank Chase has had it. He's going back to Blighty.'

'I'm glad to hear it. How did you fix it?'

'I didn't have to. I was down on the range with the Old Man. I'd told Frank to take some of the new chaps and teach them a bit of fire discipline. He got a section of them down on the ground, and ordered rapid fire. They opened up, and he opened fire with them, and then he began to spew. He was lying there on the ground, firing like mad, you could see he didn't know what he was doing, and all the noise of rapid fire in his ears, and he was spewing all over his hands and the breech of his rifle. I got him up on his feet and hustled him away before the rookies cottoned on, and I told MacAra to take over. Frank was shaking like a leaf. I stuck a fag in his mouth and lit up for him.

He could hardly hold it, poor chap. The Old Man was very nice to him, sat him in his jeep and said take it easy, and then he drove him down to the MO. I didn't go down with them, but we just got a 'phone call at the company office—Frank's excused all duties till he gets a medical board, then of course they'll send him home.'

I was relieved to hear this. For the three years that we had known Frank Chase, he had been a dependable soldier and a good comrade. But now, at the end of it all, I was coming to realise that to sustain himself in our midst had cost him more than we had known—'eating his own insides,' Trower once called it. Now he was empty.

It was not that his war experiences had been particularly bad, or that he had suffered more than his share of hardships. No single incident had given him one of those shocks that jarred so many men out of true. Probably his own physical experiences had affected him little, except to lower his resistance; it was his silent brooding over the sufferings of others that had bled him of his strength. And also that accursed conscience of his, that stubbornly prying intellect, had given him no peace. Time and again I, or some other friend, had said, 'Why don't you take it easy, Frank?' or 'You won't put the world right by worrying.' But Frank imagined himself born to put the world right by worrying.

He had political theories which gripped him with the force of religious mania; but more and more, as he absorbed experience, he found it difficult to reconcile real life and his holy dogmas. He was threatened with the loss of belief, and looking back, I believe that this was the real destroying tension in him.

He had come amongst us as one of those 'progressives' who are inspired by an over-simplified belief in human perfectibility; who believe that a few generations of reform will purge humanity of all its immemorial faults and produce a race of angels. It had been painful, then, for Frank, who had an advanced education but no schooling in life, to discover, in six years of war, how close man still is to the other animals, how savage, depraved, treacherous, filthy and invincibly stupid he can be, and how long, agonised and doubtful must be his struggle to change for the better.

Theories could no longer comfort him, for he had learned how childishly optimistic political thinking turns out to be, in the cold light of experience.

And, worst of all, although he had discovered, together with all the defects, noble and heroic qualities in the human race in greater measure than he had imagined possible, he had not discovered them among his former fellow enthusiasts, who, viewed from a distance, showed up as glib, shabby and often cowardly people to whom he did not want to return.

As long as the war was in full swing, absorption in the job, and his furious sense of responsibility, kept him intact. Now we were idle, the stretched fibres could go loose with the strain removed, and he was free to stare his own bankruptcy in the face.

I had been watching him for weeks. The symptoms, after all, were familiar. He would be silent for long periods, but would explode into little angry outbursts about nothing. He would be reckless of his own safety and of the lives of others, jeering at them as cowards if they protested. He went for days without sleep, and the most frightening thing was that he felt no exhaustion, but an unnatural brightness. He told me later that during this period he felt as if there was an intolerable storing-up of energy going on in him. After several nights without sleep, the daylight would become dazzling against his eyes, and when he tried to close them they hurt as if splinters held the lids apart. He lost his appetite and often, after forcing himself to eat a meal, or even merely to sit at table amid the smell of warm food, had to hurry away and be sick.

It was at this point that Sergeant Craig intervened. Frank went before a medical board, was down-graded, and came back to us to await his transfer.

We congratulated him on his good fortune, but our well-meaning remarks only drew from him smouldering, disbelieving looks. In his own mind, he had failed. He had wanted to be like the others, to go through to the end of the experience, and then to be able to outgrow it. It did not console him that he had been through all that mattered of the war. His will, and his flesh, had broken down while the rest of us were still on our feet; therefore he saw himself as shamefully inferior. Perhaps he suspected us of pitying him, perhaps of despising him. If so, he was wrong. But we could not tell him so, for he crouched away from us like a dog at the back of its kennel, snarling at anyone who approached.

When the day came for him to leave us, he tried to slink away like a man in disgrace. He did not say good-bye to the platoon or to his officer. I was waiting for him, with Corporal MacAra, when he came out of his hut. He looked at us. I thought he was going to say something bitter. Then his expression lowered and he said, almost inaudibly, 'Well, I'm off.'

I said, 'We'll walk up to the transport park with you.' I took Frank's pack and MacAra his rifle, and we fell in on each side of him.

We were passing the administrative buildings when we heard a shout. Sergeant Craig had appeared in a doorway, and was waving. He began to run in our direction, and I was astonished at the expression of fear and misery that appeared on Frank's face.

Sergeant Craig reached us, glowing after the run. Frank turned to face him, standing upright, arms hanging loosely at his side with the fists clenched. His face was drawn and defiant, like that of a man glaring back at his accuser. He and the sergeant faced each other like sickness and health. The sergeant said, 'Here, you weren't going off without saying good-bye?'

Frank did not answer.

Unperturbed, Craig smiled at him. 'I'd give my gratuity to be in your shoes, I can tell you. I say, if you end up anywhere near Trowbridge, will you call on my missus for me?'

Frank, whose silence now seemed to derive from a paralysis of the throat rather than from sullenness, forced an answer harshly out. 'If I get a chance.'

The sergeant held out a piece of paper. 'Thanks. I'd be grateful. An' I know she'll make you welcome. Here's the address. I'd like you to have it anyway. A friend's a friend, an' it doesn't pay to lose one.'

Frank took the paper and put it in his pocket.

Craig held out his hand. 'You've been a good NCO. I shall miss you. Get well and come back, eh?'

The firm handshake roused Frank. With a smile that was at once painful and relieved, he said, 'I'd like to. Good-bye.'

For the rest of our walk to the transport park he was silent once more; but although there was still distress in his face, we could see no bitterness. He shook hands with us like a friend, and promised to write.

He kept his word, and his letters told us the rest of his story. He went to a transit camp in Surrey. He was lonely and unhappy there, but found a surprising consolation in one fact: that the camp was full of men in the same position as him. It was staffed by 'fought-out' NCOs of the Highland Division. It was strange, he wrote, to see these fine, sturdy men strutting about the camp and parading the village with martial confidence, and to know that they, too, were used-up men. Also, there were hundreds of men sent back from overseas, lean, shabby and warlike, their eyes darkly pouched with exhaustion. Some of them, trying to conceal the same feeling of failure that troubled him, swaggered ridiculously, bragging about their experiences wherever they went; others—usually, he wrote, the men with the best personal records or from the best best units—became mulish, shameless, slouching malingerers. They would talk to no one except men who wore the same ribbons as themselves, and to these they would avow that 'they're not getting any more out of me, I can tell you'.

The officers whose job it was to find new postings for these men—mostly in the same case themselves—were sympathetic, and after a few weeks they sent Frank to take charge of the office at a supply depot near London. He was made a sergeant, and was told, 'It ought to do you good. The job's cushy, it's the kind of thing that'll interest an intelligent chap like you, and it's not far from London, so you can get up to town and drop back into the swim of things.'

To a man in Frank's state, peace and quiet can be as stunning as an explosion. He discovered this at the depot. All around, a flat plain of cornfields and water-meadows stretched like a floor beneath the immense sky. A vast, tender silence, and the vast, radiant light of summer lay upon the countryside. His mind reeled beneath the silence. He looked up at the sky and felt drowned in the light. He seemed as tiny as an insect, and lost.

He was too bewildered to fight against his loneliness. He did not visit London. It was only to the immediate past, to us, that his memory was able to reach. Peacetime had passed out of his life. He was afraid to go to London in search of the ends of long-broken threads. He wandered about in a daze, hardly aware of anything that happened except the arrival of letters from his old comrades. He hugged these to him, for they were the raw material of dreams, daydreams that burst inside him like magnesium flares, illuminating with brief, ghostly intensity the supreme experiences he had lived through. Of course, he made no new friends. He could not understand the men at the depot, and they could not understand him.

I was not surprised when he wrote that he had collapsed, and had been sent to a psychiatric hospital. I thought that he might be ashamed of this, but it was evident from his letters that his only feeling was of relief.

In the hospital he found a hiding-place from the practical problems of living, and a community which was a sort of parody of the battalion he had left behind him. The patients were all men with good records. Outwardly robust, inwardly disorganised, they hung about in groups reminiscing of old battles, rest periods in Cairo or Brussels, women, troopships, legendary brigadiers and other nostalgic topics. They talked in voices black with resentment about the 'civvy street' that lay in wait outside the hospital. Night after night they would talk; their voices would become reckless and the wards would ring with their loud, broken laughter.

He made several friends. They, like Frank himself, were all pleasant, normal-looking young men who only occasionally, in some revealing moment, would give a glimpse of their secret wounds.

There was Robbie, a corporal from Burma, who was in charge of the dramatic society and who would have passed anywhere as the life of the party. No one seeing him in the street could have guessed that he was sick. But, from time to time, he would glance at the back of his hands. Whatever he was talking about, his voice would become strained. Then the shadow would pass over and his voice become normal again. Once he clenched his fist, looked at his knuckles and said, 'Look how white they are.'

Frank said, 'What's that supposed to signify?'

'Show me yours.'

Frank clenched his fist.

Robbie said, 'Your skin isn't as white as mine.'

One day he confessed to Frank—he had a secret fear, which he could not uproot, that he had leprosy. The doctors had proved to him that he was in perfect bodily health. He knew that his obsession was nonsensical. He forbade himself to think or talk about it. But it lurked in him, refusing to be expelled.

There was Mick the parachutist, one of a group in whom the need for excitement persisted like a drug habit. They were sociable and exuberant, but they were all liable to become violently quarrelsome without apparent provocation. They got into fights, stole trifles from shops for the thrill of it, climbed out of top-storey windows to spend their nights wandering abroad, and they had a particular habit when they were together of 'bailing out' from the platform of a fast-moving cross-country bus, rolling away one after another into the gutter while one of them, acting as jump-master, counted them away, 'One, two, three, four...!'

David was an infantry sergeant, back from Italy, who could not keep awake. Whenever he stopped talking or moving for a few minutes—in buses, in the doctor's consulting-room, in the bathroom, at the dining table—he fell asleep. He had been put to sleep under drugs for days at a time; he had rested for weeks; but his condition did not change. It was as if he had gone beyond merely being exhausted, and had become exhaustion personified.

And there was Martin, a former tank commander in the desert, a tall man with a splendid, intelligent face. After his wounds had healed, he had been discharged from the Army; and as soon as he had put on a civilian suit he had collapsed. He had been brought back to hospital, given a further period of rest and sent home again. He collapsed again. In uniform he was a whole man, out of it a wreck. The hospital, for him, was a prison with an open door.

Frank was interested in his friends, and his doctor encouraged him to think about them. This was typical of the doctor's tactics towards him. There was nothing dramatic in Frank's treatment, although he wrote about it later with gratitude. The doctor did not encourage him to lay bare his sex life, recount his battle experiences or delve into his childhood. He seemed to be more concerned to turn Frank's attention outward, and to put an end to the inward monologue which Frank had been living for the last year.

He asked Frank's opinion of the hospital administration, provoked him to argue about items in the newspapers, casually encouraged him to go to concerts, plays and dances, and persuaded him to take up carpentry.

He discovered what Frank's political and philosophical outlook had been at the beginning of the war, and how distressed Frank was at the confusion into which his ideas had now dissolved. He did not sympathise with Frank, or permit him to think of himself as unfortunate, but attacked him intellectually, laughing at him, accusing him of being unable to face life without throwing away the crutch of consoling but outgrown ideas, and forcing Frank to define and clarify what experience had taught him instead of letting it gather like a fog inside his head. Merely to argue was a cure for Frank, to be forced to fight against another mind that was better trained and better in quality than his own. It was more tiring than manual labour, but his mind cleared and his spirits rose.

Probably the most valuable part of Frank's activity at this time was his study of the other patients. He discerned his own problems in them. He realised that he was not alone, an inferior, but was passing through the same crisis as many others; and the detached, sometimes amused mood with which he observed them prevented him from considering his own identical difficulties introspectively, over-solemnly or with self-pity.

Perhaps the doctor knew this when one day—Frank had then been nearly three months in the hospital—he asked Frank what he thought about Martin.

'It's obvious,' Frank answered, with all the conceit of the layman who has read a little Freud. 'The chap thinks he's a bloody hero, but he's not. He was willing to go through campaigns with other men, but he's afraid to go on through life on his own. Don't you agree?'

The doctor smiled. 'In some ways. And now, tell me, what about you?'

'What do you mean?'

The doctor closed Frank's folder. 'Send the next chap in, will you? I'll see you again tomorrow.'

The next morning Frank came into the consulting-room, sat down looking aggressive and asked, 'When are you going to let me out of here?'

'As soon as you like.'

Frank was taken aback by this answer. 'Am I better, then?'

'I imagine so.'

'Then why didn't you let me go before?'

'You didn't ask before.' A little later the doctor said, 'Tell me, do you want to be returned to your unit, or do you want your ticket?'

'You're not so bright for a doctor. Did you ever know a soldier who said "no" to his discharge?'

The doctor mused over Frank's folder. 'Good enough. It was a silly question, but I earn my living asking them.'

Frank went home a fortnight later, and a month after his discharge he was teaching at school again. He was willing now to face life as a series of campaigns from which there is no relief this side of the grave, and most of which have to be fought alone. He was not ashamed of his crisis, even though his comrades, men of a different constitution, had not undergone it as openly. His final comment to me was that, while he was going through it, he thought it was a disintegration, but looked at in retrospect it was a maturing, as messy and painful as a childbirth: the birth, that every man had to go through, of his post-war self.

One episode remains to be told. I did not hear it from him until I met him again, a year after the war.

He had been talking about himself, and the conversation had lagged. We went on to talk about other people. Frank, fittingly enough, made a reference to the man whose portrait I have drawn, to create perspective, behind this story—Sergeant Craig. 'That was a good man,' he said. 'Do you know, I think I'd nominate him as the most admirable person I met in the whole affair.'

'You know, politically, you and he were on opposite sides of the barricades.'

'It doesn't matter. I believe now that you must look for the people rather than the ideas.' He laughed. 'I don't suppose he could have thought much of me.'

'You're quite wrong. I saw him on his demob leave. He talked about you with great respect. Partly it was because you were "an educated chap". But he also said you were a real trier.'

'What's he doing now?'

'Setting up type.'

'He must be finding it hard to settle down.'

'On the contrary. He's the one chap I know who'll have been able to put the war right out of his mind and be as happy as a sandboy digging his garden.'

'That man will always be happy,' Frank said. 'I wonder why.'

He waited, but I did not utter my answer although it was, and still is, in my mind.

'I wonder what he'd have said,' Frank went on, 'if he'd been where I was the night it all ended? I never told you, did I, how I finally landed in hospital? Do you remember the night the Germans surrendered? What did they call it?—VE Night, or Victory Night, or something. That was the night I collapsed.'

He worked all day in the depot office, while a babble of talk went on around him. The other clerks were comparing their prospects for demobilisation, exchanging rumours, making jubilant plans to celebrate. Frank remained silent. He felt as if the world had stopped spinning.

In the evening, all the other men in the billet went out. Frank remained behind, and tried to settle down with a book in the deserted room. He was eaten up with unrest, and was assailed by a strange panic as if he were about to die. The print made him giddy. He put the book away. He was afraid to go to bed before the other men came back. He was fighting to drive off a flock of black thoughts that were flapping and swooping about him like night-birds. In bed, in the silence, they might overwhelm him. He went for a walk.

He walked along the village street. He gave himself up to dreams. This was always the easiest escape for him. It was so easy, and so comforting, to let the street become the street of a Norman village. Instead of the metalled surface beneath his feet he saw a white, unpaved roadway in front of him. Instead of the little shops and red-brick houses on either side of him, he saw greystone cottages with shellholes gaping in their steep roofs. The radiant, liquid moonlight of a vanished summer poured down on the imagined scene. He was on his own. The rest of the patrol was waiting in the shadows, fifty yards behind, for his signal to come on. The village was silent. He could hear no sign of life. Were the enemy here? He watched the empty windows and the shadowed doorways with the intentness of a man whose life depends upon it. He walked with a cat's tread. He gripped his carbine across his breast so tightly that his wrists hurt. There was a constriction, like the pressure of a single finger, at the base of his windpipe. He knew that feeling. Excitement? Fear? It was the feeling of being alive for the first time in his life.

A flare soared into the sky in front of him. He looked up as the little white ball spread into a shimmer of light, that ghostly flarelight which is no more than a luminous veil drawn across the darkness for a few seconds. And he thought he had gone mad. For he could see the flare, he could really see it.

He stood with the village behind him and dark fields lying before him. From the distance, in the darkness, he heard a vague hallooing, and a faint red glow stained the night. Then there was the rush of rockets, and signals—

German signals—began to burst high above him, red and green flares sailing slowly into the dark sky. And then slamming explosions, each with its flash of white light upon the ground, and the detonations hitting inside his body. Where was he? Had he finally lost himself between dream and reality? He walked on, trembling, trying to keep a hold on himself.

The red glow in the night grew brighter. Yellow and scarlet flames leaped up. They lit up the wide field in front of him. He saw the hedges, the gates, and found his bearings. Across behind the hedge was the dump. There was a supply of captured German ammunition kept there. He could see the bonfire now, and the leaping human shapes around it. They were having their victory celebration.

He was still standing at the gate when the public-house closed and discharged a fresh contingent to join in the frolic. The whooping and screaming, which up till now had been echoing faintly across the fields, burst out behind him. He looked round and saw a stream of people pouring out of the village street. They came pouring past him, jostling him aside, and flung open the five-barred gate to swarm into the field.

They were leaping and dancing, arms linked, hands joined, men and women clutching each other round the waist or clinging round each other's necks. The faces streamed past him, faces for a Breughel, red and ugly with drink, the fat faces of ale-wives glistening with the distant firelight, the suet-lump faces of men who had not been judged young or intelligent enough to die, the vacuous whore-faces, pathetically greedy for pleasure, of little village girls. They squealed and shrieked, filled the night with graceless laughter, bawled idiot songs, coughed, screamed, yelled and belched. The women kicked up their legs and threw up their skirts, prancing about in a kind of lewd madness. The mooing herd poured past Frank, and he hated them. They were the first people in the whole war whom he had truly hated.

The soldiers were setting off thunderflashes as they ran, throwing them to right and left. Between the walls of the back lanes they burst with violent detonations. Each explosion was a stunning blow to Frank, shaking his senses more and more.

A woman reeled past, a stout, middle-aged housewife, with two soldiers hanging upon her like dogs trying to pull her down. She was panting, 'Come on, come on, boys,' trying to lead them towards the celebration while they were striving to pull her aside, out of the stream of people, into the dark and lonely field. The three of them swayed and tugged, in a confused group, in front of Frank. The men uttered no sound but canine grunts. The woman sent flight after flight of breathless laughter into the night, her panting growing louder and quicker. Then, in a fat voice that was pregnant with giggles, she cried out, 'Oh, we've had some fun these last few years, haven't we, boys?' She let the men drag her off into the darkness, and as she lurched away between them, Frank heard her voice, high and hideously girlish, once more, 'Oh, well, all good things must come to an end, worse luck!'

Frank turned away from the gate and began to walk back towards the billet. His head was ringing with the woman's last words. They had broken the seals he was trying to keep on his mind, and all his thoughts were pouring forth. The whole war came back to him, all the worst of it, all the stunned, uncomprehending eyes of wounded men, the sweet smell of dead flesh rotting in the sun, the light-headed, burning clarity of sleeplessness, fear's clutch at the bowels, the torturing weight of pack and weapons after hours of marching, the misery of dysentery and malaria, the deadness of legs knee-deep in icy Flanders water, the terrible discovery that six irrecoverable years of life had vanished like a day, and his old, always returning question, 'What for, what for, what for?' And through it all, he could hear the drunken female voice, 'All good things must come to an end, worse luck!'

A thunderflash exploded at his feet, and he cried out, throwing his arms up in front of his face. A beery voice shouted, 'Windy!' Somebody else threw another firework, and another explosion rocked him. He reeled away, clinging to his last reserves of intelligence in order to reach the billet, while at his heels the thunderflashes burst, and the crowd shrieked with laughter, yelling derision at him, driving him off like an unwelcome ghost who had tried to return from the nether world.

He was shaking from head to foot, and his legs were like lead, when he entered the empty barrack-room. He fell across his bed, face downwards, and began to laugh. He laughed for a long time, until he was exhausted. When the other men came back they found him there, unable to move. The next day he was taken to hospital.

'Craig would have laughed too,' I said, when Frank had finished his story.

'But not like me,' Frank said.

Manners Makyth Man

I was on my own, one sunny afternoon in the spring of nineteen forty-five, in a provincial town. As the blue bands on the epaulettes of my battledress showed, I was on pass from hospital. I had another eight hours of liberty. I was tired after wandering about. The streets were deserted. All the shops were closed. I could see nothing but row after row of doors shut and blank against the stranger. In despair, I asked a passer-by where the nearest cinema was. He told me, and was about to walk on when he said, 'They don't open for above two hours. Would you like to come home to tea?'

He was a short, sturdy man, wearing his Sunday suit and a clean cloth cap. As we walked, he told me that he worked in a foundry. He was out for his weekly smell of fresh air. It tasted like sherbert after six days shut up with the furnaces. He had just been to the recreation ground to feed the birds. 'It sounds daft,' he said apologetically, 'but if you knew what the noise was in the shop, you'd want to do something like that once in a while.'

He lived in one of those little brick boxes, each with a scrubbed sunken doorstep, which are joined in their monotonous hundreds to make monotonous hundreds of streets in a hundred factory towns. The street door opened directly into a living-room, small, spotless and full of furniture, with a big kitchen range that gleamed with blacklead. He introduced me to his wife. 'This is Joan. This is Alex. He's been kind enough to come and keep us company.' She greeted me with a frank, unsurprised air, made me comfortable and said, 'You'll be wanting a cup of tea.'

After the introductory cup we talked. They asked me no questions, but talked about the foundry, their married children, and what diversions I might find in the town on a weekday. Dennis, the husband, wanted to know if I was interested in the local football team. I said that I usually went into Birmingham on Saturday to follow the Villa. Joan left us to talk football and laid the table with a spotless white cloth, a rose-painted tea service and a set of gleaming cutlery. Then we had tea, a big meal with a fresh loaf from which Dennis cut me inch-thick slices, smoked haddock served swimming in melted butter, a cut-glass dish of jam full of real strawberries and a home-baked fruit cake. After tea John lit the fire that was already laid in the grate, and soon a great red bank of coals was blazing behind the bars. I sat in an armchair at the fireside, smoking a cigarette. Joan said, 'Shut your eyes if you want to. Don't mind us.' I answered that I was not tired but—out of sheer contentment, I think—fell asleep.

When I awoke the electric light was on, and some neighbours were just coming in for the evening; an elderly couple, their daughter and her boyfriend. Dennis introduced me. 'This is Alex, a friend of ours.' The evening passed happily.

I was afraid, when the time came for me to leave, that Dennis would offer me money. It sometimes happened in cases like this. I felt that if he should do so, it would be more considerate to accept than to refuse, but I felt guilty at the idea, for I had returned from abroad with sixty pounds back pay to my account and this seemed to me such staggering and unsurpassable wealth that I ought not to take money from a working man.

Dennis walked up to the bus stop with me. He made no attempt to press money on me. Before I boarded the bus we shook hands and he said, 'I hope you'll give us the pleasure of coming again. You won't be shy, will you?'

I promised to come again and waved good-bye as the bus moved off.

I sat down and put my hand in my pocket for the fare. Under my handkerchief I found a spill of stiff paper. I took it out. It was a ten-shilling note, carefully folded.

Scum of the Earth

'**S**cum o' the earth!'

Everybody in the bar turned to look at the man who had spoken. He was leaning forward, pressing down on the counter with his two hands, his head turned as if to challenge all of us. He was an elephant of a man, bulking above those around him so that they looked like sycophants. He had a square head and no visible neck. His face was unhealthily purple, shot with hairlike red veins, with a small nose set in the middle of it beneath pale blue eyes. In tweeds, and sober, he might have passed for a farmer come to market. But he was drunk; the belligerent bellow in his voice, addressed not to the chance companion he had been talking to but to the company at large, testified to that; and he was in khaki. He looked absurd, swaying to and from the counter with his battleblouse unfastened and his great sagging belly trying to burst out of his trousers; all the more absurd because his hair was cropped from the neck to the crown of his head, with only a ragged schoolboy fringe protruding over his forehead. In repose, the wide face with its small nose and mouth must have had a babyish vacuity, but now the blind, metallic gleam of aggression in the pale eyes made it ugly.

'Scum o' the earth, them Wops is.' It must have been the upthrust of savagery in him, released by drink, that had made him turn from his companion to shout at the rest of us. 'You know what I seen them Eyetalians do? I seen 'em eating out o' dustbins. That's what I seen 'em do.'

He glared around at us, angrily triumphant as if he had uttered a revelation. He lifted another pint glass to his mouth. He had a row of them on the counter in front of him, several already empty, some still full and frothing. As he drank we could see the quartermaster's insignia on his sleeve.

'Ah!' He wiped his mouth and set the glass down. 'I'll lower all this lot afore you've finished a fag. That's what I've set 'em up for. Takes ten pints to make a man, they say. Me, man-and-'alf, I am. You'll see! Fifteen pints and not a hiccup, that's me. Ah,' he repeated. 'Eating out o' dustbins. Crusts, lumps o' fat we'd chewed and spat out, swill, anything. That's the Eyetalians for you.'

He looked down at the little man next to him as if he had been challenged. 'I know!' he said belligerently. 'Think I'm a liar?' The poor man had not uttered a word. 'Two years I had out there. Two stinking horrible years in the middle of 'em. Wops wherever you went, swarmed like bloody flies they did. Allied Force Headquarters, that's where I was, while you lot was having it cushy in Blighty.

'Listen to this! I come out of my tent one night. I hears something scraping away round the swillbins. What is it? Rats? I likes a bit o' sport going after rats. So I picks up a lump o' wood and I goes round to have a look.'

He lowered his head for a moment, collecting himself for the effort of further coherent speech. He emptied another glass, sighed harshly with pleasure and went on, no longer shouting but speaking with a sustained stridency. 'Know what it was grubbin' in them swillbins? I'll tell yer. It was a kid. One o' them Eyetie girls. Fifteen year old. No more than that. Not a day more. Fifteen year old, and there she was grubbin' like a pig in the swillbin. That's a country for yer! That's the way they bring their kids up!

'I stood there and I watched her for a minute. We'd chucked some rotten cheese away. Green, it was! 'Orrible! She was stuffin' it into her mouth with both hands. And she had a bag. One o' them women's bags. She was puttin' stuff into it. Muck, swill, it turned your guts up to see.'

He paused for another drink, caught sight of himself in the mirror and gave his image a lowering grin. 'Ha! I stepped out on her, caught her arm, you should a' seen her jump! "What you doin' here?" White as a sheet she was. I could feel her little thin arm shaking. She stood there jabberin' away at me.

'"Get out," I says. "Imshi. Vada via!" She drops her bag, and she puts her hands together, you'd think she was praying. Ah, they're crafty little bitches, them Eyeties. No one to beat 'em for gettin' round you, not even the Wogs, an' I've kicked a few of them around in my time, I can tell you. She stands there with her face turned up, and her hands lifted up to me as if I was the Virgin Mary, and tears runnin' down her cheeks. "Let me stay," she says. "Let me take food. For mamma," she says, "for bambini"—all that kind of yap. Me, I can understand her. I speak the lingo. Smart chap I am, couple o' years out there, a smart chap catches on to the lingo. "Go on," I says. "Blow! Beat it!" And I gives her a clout round the face. Only way with them Eyeties.

Ah, same as the Wogs they are, it's no use talkin' to 'em, it's only your fist they understand.

'No use. Stubborn as mules when they're after something. I tell you, scum, they are! So I says, "Listen, you want food?" She nearly nods her scabby head off. "Come on, then," I says, and I grabs her arm and I yanks her into my tent.

'Ah! Dunno what I wasted my time with her for! Place like that, you can get the best there is for a tin o' beef. I've had a few! Her—there wasn't enough of her to make twopenn'orth o' broth. Skin an' bones, that's all she was. Little thin thing, hadn't the strength to strike a match. Ha, I give her what for! I taught her what you get for beggin'! I flattened her into that bed till she was black in the face. I wrung her out between these bloody hands of mine like a wet handkerchief. Ah, I taught her a lesson, all right. I made her sorry she'd ever been born.

'And d'you think she struggled? D'you think she tried to get away? Nah, not her! Pride? Self-respect? They've never heard of it, them Eyeties. The things she let me do to 'er! Filthy, she was! That's the only word for it, filthy! Anything I told her, she done it. Never a bloody protest. Nah, not them! I made her—wah, I tied her up in knots, I did. She couldn't move when I'd finished with her. I had to throw her out. I had to chuck her out of that tent like a scruffy sick cat. What's that? Nah, never done her no harm. They're born to it, like animals, you can't hurt 'em, they're bred to it from the cradle. She just crawled off and—ah, this'll show you what they're like—'

He emptied another glass and belched. 'Know what?' His voice rose again to a triumphant, demonstrative bellow, the words thickly articulated but still distinct and coherent. 'Same time next night, back she comes. Of her own free will. That's the Wops for yer. Wha'd I tell yer? Shameless, stinkin' scum, that's all they are. Straight to my tent, she comes, and she pulls her dress off, and she sits on the bed, and off we go, the same old bloody performance as the night before. And when I've finished she points to the swillbins and she says, "Can I take now?" Always on the cadge, them.'

Another glass of beer: he was swaying. He kept lifting his head as if it were a great burden, his lips were slack and his eyes, their lids weighted by the drink, were going dull. His words became more and more slurred, and his voice kept bursting out and recovering as if, like his body, it was swaying every moment towards his listeners. Nevertheless he was still speaking clearly, in the dogged, mournful, lecturing tone of the drunk. 'Here, see this? The last glass. Fifteen pints! Gentlemen here said he'd pay for 'em if I could drink 'em. Got your money ready, mister?

'Here, wait, ah, wait, I haven't finished telling you. This tart. Every night, regular as clockwork, along she come with her shopping-bag. Into me tent she come, then off she went to the swillbins. Ha, she got her swill all right, but I made her earn it.' He was mumbling now, hardly able to move his lips, and people were losing interest. His head swung slowly from side to side, staring at the last glass that stood before him on the counter. His eyes opened wide as if he were trying to remember the rest of his story. 'I made her earn it. Something for nothing, that's all they want. Wops, always after something for nothing. Don't get something for nothing off me. I ain't no Wop. I'm British. British! Made her earn it, that's what I did. Taught her tricks. I taught her tricks like a little puppy dog. All scabby skin and bones. Put your fingers round her waist. That's how thin she was. That's how thin. I let her feel my weight. I'm a big feller, I am, here, look, you can see, I'm a big feller, I am. Anything I said, she done it. Not a scrap o' shame in 'em. Dirty minds, dirtiest bloody minds in the world, them women. Whores. Born whores, every mother's one of them. Whores. They're all whores in It'l—' the liquid consonant was too much for him, and he broke off.

He finished off the last glass. 'There she goes! No better than animals. Gotta keep 'em in their places. 'S wha' they're there for. Gorrabekept—' he swayed, and almost fell. Suddenly he shouted, 'Scum o' the earth! I seen 'em! They're all the same, Wops and Wogs, all them niggers and Chinks. Scum o' the earth!'

His legs buckled under the massive weight of his body and he fell to the floor with a great soft thump. Nobody moved to help him. He raised himself on his hands and, there on all fours like a beast, glared around him. He opened his mouth to speak, but a horrible gurgling noise burst out of him, and the bar filled with a sour stench as he vomited upon the floor.

The Way a War Ends

I suppose it is not hard to understand why the word 'Berlin' meant so much to us. Our life before the war, and our youthful ambitions, had faded from our memories. The ideals—or illusions, call them what you like—which had been held up to us at the beginning of it all, were forgotten. The whole thing had become a drudgery.

In nineteen forty-five, my friends and I were separated. Units were being disbanded, men were being sent to the Far East or to garrisons in Germany. I had been injured in a road accident and posted home.

'Berlin'—the word symbolised the only hope that we held on to at the end of the war. The old hopes had died, but a new one had appeared since nineteen forty-one, as the Red Army had marched westward. 'Joe's boys.' Every soldier admired them, talked about them. They embodied every miracle that we prayed for: something new, something strong, the old muddlers thrown out and people like ourselves doing the big things. We had travelled up through Italy, landed in Normandy, campaigned through France and the Low Countries with the same vague but burning vision in all our minds: of another army, made up of young men like ourselves, suffering the same hardships and dangers as ourselves, and bringing their great secret to share with us: an army of young men with red stars on their helmets coming to meet us from the East.

The worse everything else became, the more of the old lies that we saw through, the more sick and tired we became, the more fiercely we nourished within ourselves a dream: of brothers coming face to face and taking the future out of the hands of those who might ruin it. And the place of that encounter would be—Berlin.

I waited to hear from Ted Trower. He had gone, as a driver, to a motorised battalion in an armoured division. They had been chosen for a place of honour in the Berlin garrison. And Ted, more than any of us, had taken the Russians to his heart.

Perhaps it was not strange that this should have happened to the one man among us who proclaimed a militant belief in nothing. There was a vacuum to be filled. He listened devoutly, with brooding, burning eyes, to Frank Chase's lectures about Russia. He borrowed books from me: for I had shared the enthusiasm. He would not argue with heretics; he would listen to them, tense and smouldering; he would tell them, sharply, to shut up; or he would use his fists.

The rest of us were out of the running, but Ted, at least, would enjoy the big moment. Perhaps through his letters I would be able to share in it.

His first letter was about the ceremonial entry of the battalion into Berlin. There was no elation—I had not expected any—only a grumble about the extra drills, 'tailor's parades' and blancoing involved.

After a few weeks another letter came. He was having a good time. The chaps could get anything they liked for soap and cigarettes. The black market was a real eye-opener. I was missing something, not being there. He had a wonderful wrist-watch for his wife. Did I want a Leica? He'd bring one back for me. There were lashings of drink. He supposed I'd heard about the girls. It was all true about them, they were the easiest he'd ever come across in his life, especially the married ones still waiting for their husbands. They were good-lookers too. You only had to whistle and they all came running. Only you had to be careful, Berlin was crawling with the pox. He was doing all right. He was ashamed to take his shirt off in front of the lads, his girl had bit him to pieces. He went on to describe how she made love.

I was faintly surprised at this. Ted had been fond of his wife. In two years' campaigning he had, for the most part, kept contemptuously away from women. In any case, neither of us had ever troubled to talk much about our occasional private adventures: certainly not in this tone of overexcited relish, nor in such detail. However, I was not moved to pass any mental judgement.

He had not mentioned the subject I wanted to hear about. I wrote, 'What about the Russians?'

A week later I received his reply. The first words were, 'Those bastards?' He went on, after a long dash scored across the page, 'Listen, when we marched in we took over a cavalry barracks from them. We were all shined up, the old man in front looking pleased with himself. We were all set for the usual exchange of compliments, you know, them turning out the guard for us, us marching past eyes right, all that sort of bull. Well, when we got there the last of them were just trailing off, scruffy, shambling great ruffians all loaded up with every kind of civvy loot under the sun. They had their backs to us. The few that looked round didn't even give us a wave. None of their officers came out to meet us.

'Then we went inside. Now listen to this. They're not soldiers. They can't be bloody human, those bastards. They're pigs, that's what they are, pigs on their hind legs. They'd crapped on the floor, in the same rooms they'd slept in. Look, old soldier, I'm not kidding, in the same rooms they'd slept in, ate in too for all I know. I tell you, some of the lads just stood there and spewed their hearts up at the smell of it.'

A fresh page. 'We had to change into our denims out in the yard, and unpack mops and buckets off the transport, and we spent the whole day scrubbing the whole place out from top to bottom, and burning the straw they'd left, and squirting DDT around, and swilling all the floors with carbolic, before we could move in.

'Think of it. This battalion came all the way from Africa, two thousand miles of bloody misery, all those good chaps buried on the way, and what for? To clean their crap up after them!'

That was all he said about the Russians. But, holding his letter, I could feel the rage coming from it like body heat.

He wrote less often after that. There was more about the loot he was collecting, about methods the men had invented for smuggling it home, about his German girl, about the night clubs. Sometimes he wrote about Berlin, in a stolid, tourist fashion. There were a lot of ruins, worse than London. There were big blocks of flats where quite poor people lived. They were very modern and airy. He hadn't known that Germans lived as well as this. They were a very clean people. They were easy to get on with. They were all fed up with the war. After all, they couldn't have done anything to stop it. They were only the likes of us, and what can the likes of us do, only what we're told. And then they'd had all this propaganda pushed into them, the same as we had. They believed what they were told. But so did we, didn't we? Look what they'd told us about the wonderful Russians.

The Russians. He wrote savagely, as if he blamed me for the Russians. Your Russians, he wrote, your bloody Russians. He told me all the atrocity stories his German girl had told him. Anyone would think they'd won the war, he said in one letter, the way they swaggered around. In another letter he said, 'They won't be satisfied till they've conquered us, too.' In the very next, with a complete absence of irony, 'The old man reckons we won't be safe till we've put them out for the count like we did the bloody Jerries.'

A period of silence followed. It must have been five or six weeks. At last, in the late autumn, when the nights were growing long and cold, I heard from Ted again. There was no address at the head of his letter, no greeting, and—I glanced at the end and noticed with perplexity—no signature, but I recognised his writing.

The first page—some quirk of vanity must have inspired him to attempt dramatic effect—consisted of these words. 'Well, I've done it.'

On another sheet he continued: 'I suppose I might as well tell you. It'll give you something to think about, anyway. I was coming home late one night, it was through a poor part of Berlin, all smashed up, ruins on both sides of the street, pitch dark. I heard someone coming down the street towards me. I could hear his boots sort of crashing across the pavement, not regular, I knew it was a drunk. After a bit we came up against each other, and it was a Russian.

'Well, there we are on the pavement. He's waiting for me to walk round him, and I'm waiting for him to walk round me. I'd had a few drinks myself, I was just about fit for a bit of trouble. He's a young chap, about my size, fair hair all messed up. He's wearing one of these long greatcoats. I tell him to stand aside. He doesn't answer for a minute, then he starts shouting at me, glaring at me like mad, and I answer him back. Neither of us can understand a blind word of what the other one is saying. Then he tries to shove me out of the way. And I shove him back. And all of a sudden it comes on me, this is the last straw. I haven't come all this way to step off the pavement, not to Jesus Christ Almighty Himself. So I try to push on past him. And he catches my arm, and he shouts into my face, and he tries to shake me. Blazing angry, he is. Then he reaches with his other hand, quick as lightning, into his coat pocket.'

As I read I had a vision of the two young men who had come 'all this way' to face each other, as alike, as close, and as eternally apart as one man and his image in a mirror. 'Well, you know what it's been like here. I've told you. Street fights galore. We're not allowed to carry weapons out of barracks, they're afraid of shootings. But us chaps are all wise to it. We all carry knives. Safest thing. I haven't come all this way to cop it off some bloody Russian.

'Well, I see him go for whatever he's got, and my guts turn over, and before I know, my knife's in my hand and I've let him have it. A quick short one upwards, right between the ribs.

'Well, the Russian goes down and I have a look at him. Yes, he's had it all right.

'Well, I didn't know what to do for a minute. I wiped the knife on his coat and put it away. Then I had an idea. I lugged him down to the end of the street, and I filled his greatcoat pockets with bricks, and I rolled him into the Spandau Canal. He's still there, for all I know.

'Well, what do you think of that?—you and your Russians!'

I wrote to him later without referring to his letter. He did not answer me, and I never heard from him again.

That, I suppose, is how a war ends—and begins.

The Human Kind:
An Epilogue

Towards evening a mist gathered far out over the Yellow Sea. The silence, which had lain upon the sea all day, as vast and weighty as the infinite arch of sky, seemed to thicken with the mist. The red sun sank behind the skyline. Wavering faint tracks of light, filtering through the mist, billowed across the sea, then shrank and dimmed, and the waters grew dark.

Inland, where the Korean hills, themselves like a sea of grey waves mysteriously halted, ran away towards the Chinese frontier, a deeper gloom had already begun to gather, creeping forward to shorten the range of vision. The intermittent thump and grumble of artillery, which had been loud in the white light of day, was deadened in the evening, lost among the shadowed uplands, its whereabouts betrayed only by the white soft glare of gunflashes.

Casey and the new lieutenant, who had been watching the sunset from a grassy dune above the beach, heaved themselves to their feet and walked down the track which led to the camp. Neither of them spoke. The lieutenant, who had been trying to make conversation for the last hour, had at last been browbeaten into silence. He had been making his first tour of the company's rest area, with Casey, who wore a sergeant's chevrons, as his guide. From time to time Casey had spoken, briefly and expertly, but only of military matters. The lieutenant, a replacement fresh from the States, who had not yet seen action, regarded him with curiosity, with respect, and already with a touch of fear.

A faint wind stirred among the pines that grew on the slopes; somewhere a branch creaked and cracked. The lieutenant began to walk faster; the stories that he had read in the American papers of guerrillas, guerrillas everywhere, haunted his thoughts; they were north of the Parallel, enemy ground, enemy population; then he glimpsed the twist of amusement at the corners of Casey's compressed lips. He slowed down to the same unhurrying, noiseless, relaxed walk—a soldier's walk—as Casey. In every move he was now a furtive but conscious imitator. He felt foolish at having started to hurry like some small boy going alone to the movies for the first time, plunging through the frightening adult crowds with a dime clutched in a sweaty hand.

'Movies.' Casey's voice, and the word itself, stunned him. He halted. Casey studied him with a look that was absent yet contemptuously questioning. Casey motioned with his head, and the lieutenant understood. In the clearing below them an open-air film show had just begun. The screen blinked white once or twice then flickered with colour. There was a welcoming rumble of laughter from the huddle of American infantrymen who filled the clearing. 'What's 'a matter?' Casey made a jibe of every word. 'Don't ya wanna go down see th' movies?'

The lieutenant could only answer childishly, 'Sure.' He followed Casey again. In the dusk he studied his companion's face—the bitter, black eyes, the sunken cheeks fringed with stubble, the thin lips playing with a cigarette, the nose broken at the bridge as if a devil had stamped savagery into the man's face with a cloven heel. The lieutenant wondered, as he had been wondering all the afternoon, what went to the making of such a face.

'Sergeant,' he asked. 'Where you from?'

The cigarette jiggled up and down. 'Wichita, Kansas.' Casey did not look back, and there was no encouragement in his voice.

The lieutenant felt that he must persist. 'Married?'

'Naaah.'

'You got a girl?'

'Say!' Casey's lips pulled apart in the corner, and he faced the lieutenant with a restless, resentful stare. 'Whaddya...?' He checked himself and walked on until, as if driven to speak by an inner boastfulness that he could not restrain, he said: 'Back there, I got a million dames.'

They continued in silence along the path. It was Casey's walk that the lieutenant watched now. Leopards must pad through the night as this man walked. The lieutenant wondered how long it would take him to become like this. He thought about it with horror, for the shape of the old life, with a drag like a gravitational pull, was still close behind him: books on a shelf, the spray whirling on the summer lawn, the kids shrieking in pursuit of a ball, cutlery gleaming on a table, Janice in a flowered frock laughing up at him, nestling sombrely at his side in the Chev., dancing softly up against him. He thought about it with envious admiration, for the man was a complete soldier, burned black and hard, a man who had already achieved what he must yet attempt.

The lieutenant feared what lay ahead, no personal compulsion had brought him here, he had been loaded in a transport 'plane and shot across the oceans like a grain of powder in the body of a shell. Terror and bewilderment gathered in him at what had befallen him; and whenever he was on his own and trying to rest, they burst out in a great silent cry, demanding to know what he was doing here, why he could not go back. There were enemies somewhere: the only hate he had for them was that they were the reason for his being here. There were things that he was not made to do, to live without thinking, to face danger without thinking, to kill without thinking.

Casey prowled on ahead of him, the man who could do these things, the man who had been bred to live without thinking, the man who had always prowled lonely and wary as a leopard in city streets, the man who had always had to look on every other man as an enemy, to snatch and strike and pounce for his sustenance, the man who could kill the unidentified enemy in the dark: the tough guy, the killer, the hero of film and radio and great black headlines. Fear, transmuted, fed his impatience to become like Casey.

And now it was the lieutenant's dread of the silence, and what silence let loose in him, that made him try again. 'Sergeant Casey, what did you do before the war?'

The sergeant walked on for a few paces before he replied, 'Any thin' fer a buck.'

Another silence.

'And Casey, how old are you?'

A flare of suspicion in Casey's eyes. 'Twenty-four.'

The lieutenant looked helplessly away. He was twenty-six, and he had thought that the sergeant was an older man. He fumbled for a packet of Luckies and offered Casey a fresh cigarette. They lit up, between cupped hands, and moved on.

As they came nearer to the camp the pines began to thin out. A week ago, when the regiment had landed from the sea, there had been a battle here at the clearing, and before the battle there had been a village. Now the ground was cratered, diseased. Where peasant huts had stood were burned patches, with a few blackened stumps of wood protruding from the ground.

Trees lay across each other like corpses. Those that still stood were gashed and splintered, their foliage torn away and littered on the ground. Beyond the camp there were more stricken trees, then a further shallow slope, then the road they had fought to clear, then paddyfields for a mile or two till the hills began to rise.

And in the air, above the stubborn stench of burning, there was a strange sweetness, a scent which was hardly perceptible at first but which became more and more noticeable until, inexplicably, it was sickening. The lieutenant did not yet know what it was, but Casey could have told him. Most of the American dead had been stuffed into the ground days since; but there were dead peasants in the ashes of their huts and dead Korean soldiers lying in the paddyfields hidden by the tall rice-shoots; and this, the sweet and horrible smell of their corruption, rose to assail the living.

In the midst of all this the soldiers were squatting with their rifles propped between their knees, watching the film. Casey and the lieutenant were close enough to recognise Donald Duck cavorting across the screen. The noises of the evening—the distant gunfire and the sound of engines warming up on an airfield somewhere—were lost behind the surges of laughter from the audience which alternated with the raucous quacking from the amplifiers.

They stood for a while looking down at their men. The lieutenant was oppressed with despair at the failure of his friendly overtures. It seemed to him that his one great aim in life just now must be to come to terms with Casey. He tried a new approach. 'Movies, shows, do you get a lot of that kind a thing?'

'Naaah.'

'What do the fellas do when they're resting?'

Casey would rarely look at the lieutenant when he spoke. He kept his eyes on the ground in front of him, or on the vast mysterious sky, in a moody impenetrable gaze. There was never any evidence of thought, or of a human personality whose interest could be engaged, behind those eyes. 'Nuthun'. Lay aroun', I guess.'

'You, what do you do?'

Casey answered, with only a sullen contraction of the face so that the lieutenant could not guess whether he was being sarcastic, 'Look at th' funnies.'

'Yeah, but the people up here, don't you get along with the people up here?'

'People?' For the first time Casey's glance was alive, a sharp interrogative flash under hunched eyebrows. 'Ain't no people.'

'Yeah, but...'

'Gooks, theah's nuthun' else.'

The lieutenant was defeated. He dropped his butt-end, smeared it into the ground with his foot and made to move on; but Casey was staring into the trees. The cigarette which had been drooping in the corner of his mouth jerked suddenly up like the alert barrel of an anti-aircraft gun. He gripped the lieutenant's arm and, without speaking, pointed upwards.

The officer could discern nothing in the treetops for a moment; then, through the pattern of twigs and shadow and clear dusk, he saw the man; a Korean, clinging to the top of a twenty-foot pine. His heart thumped with excitement at the sight of his first live enemy, and he thought for a moment that he was going to be sick. With numbed fingers he fumbled for his automatic, before he realised that at this range it was useless.

Casey, watching the treetop intently, slowly unslung the Garand from his shoulder. He held it in readiness across his body but made no move to aim. The lieutenant, with suspense like a finger shoved down his throat, waited. 'Sniper,' he muttered.

'Little brown bastard!' Casey leaned across till his mouth was close to the officer's ear. 'Y'r glasses,' he said. He did not whisper; he had the soldier's way of talking, softer and less sibilant than a whisper.

The lieutenant remembered his field-glasses. He trained them on the crotch of the tree in which the Korean was perched. He adjusted them with unsteady fingers, so that the image in the graticuled circles of the lenses grew clear then blurred, grew clear and blurred and grew clear again until he was looking, not daring now to breathe, into the distinct face of his enemy.

'Here,' said Casey. The officer handed him the glasses. 'By God,' said Casey, 'he's laughing.'

The lieutenant took the glasses back and looked again. The Korean was looking down, towards the soldiers in the clearing, towards the screen. The lieutenant could see the brown, hard chest that the Korean's shirt, loose and dirty white, revealed, the strong bare legs. And the face—now he could make out the face, simian at first glance and grinning, but, as he studied it more closely, a peasant face with hunger and suffering indelibly written as on a palimpsest beneath each passing expression, written now on his puckered face as he grinned down at the screen.

'Bastard,' the lieutenant muttered. 'What 'n hell's he doing?' He said to Casey, 'Kill him.'

Casey did not answer.

'I said kill him. Before he kills one of our guys.'

'He ain't gotta gun.'

The lieutenant was crushed. He had been staring at the man with the eyes of a man, not with the eyes of a soldier. He had not seen what he should have seen first. Reality receded from him. He felt dizzy and remote, aching with the effort of remaining motionless and staring up into the treetop. He heard, as from miles away, echoing in some dream in which space and time reveal their infinity, the screeching loudspeakers and the answering gusts of laughter. 'He's a spy,' he murmured. 'Don't you see he's a spy? Kill him I tell you.'

Casey ignored him.

It was Casey, still self-possessed and vigilant, who saw the screen flicker and go blank as the film ended. He tugged at the lieutenant's arm and made a sign with his hand. The two men moved silently off the path and crouched behind a tree.

There was a stir among the audience. Men rose to stretch their legs. Matches flared. Casey lowered his rifle, and the cigarette in the corner of his mouth drooped again. Noiselessly, the Korean had quit his nest and was coming down the tree, quick and sinuous. He stood for a second at its foot, then he ducked away into the sparse undergrowth.

Casey looked along the sights of his rifle. His eyes were half-closed in a weary, uninterested squint. The Korean emerged from the bushes farther from the camp, and began to move, shadowlike, towards the highway. As he moved, the rifle moved with him, slowly.

The lieutenant was peering through his glasses again, straining to see clearly in the dusk. He picked up the Korean, focused, and for a second saw the man's face once more. 'Jesus!' Joy overcame him. He knew now, weak and relieved, he knew that he was not looking at an enemy. Stamped on the peasant's face was the same grin that he had seen before; there was no mistaking it, an expression of utter pleasure clung to for fear of losing it, like that of a little boy hurrying home from a movie. 'Casey, he's no spy. He's happy! He's seen the movie and he's going home.'

'Whaddya know—' Casey settled his chin against the rifle butt and looked emptily down the sights as they moved ahead of the Korean. 'Ya'd think the guy was human!'

As if reluctantly, he lowered the barrel of his rifle, and lay with his chin upon his fist, his eyes gleaming with thought.

From the City, From the Plough
Alexander Baron

introduction by Sean Longden

The story of soldiers of the Fifth Battalion, the Wessex Regiment in
the run up to and after D-Day. Although fictional, it comes directly
out of the author's own experience, and is one of the most accurate
and unsentimental portrayals of the ordinary soldier's life anywhere
in fiction. The prose is spare and crisp, the narrative voice at times
chilling, but alive to the humour and humanity of soldiers at war as
well as the conflict's ruthlessness and inhuman momentum.

"This is the only war book that has conveyed any sense of reality to me"
    V. S. PRITCHETT

*"robust and honest without being sensational, warm-hearted without being
sentimental, stimulating without being slick"*
    NEW STATESMAN

*"Every scene is alive with humour and pity, with a deep controlled fury,
with the stuff of life itself...tough, taut, yet profoundly expressive...This book
left me mentally numb for a week...Get this book and read it...insist on
having it...it is magnificent"*
    TRIBUNE

"A war book that is the real thing"
    DAILY TELEGRAPH

"A fine and moving book"
    NEW YORK TIMES

Black Spring Press • paperback • 978-0-948238-44-4 • 224pp

The Lowlife

Alexander Baron

introduction by Iain Sinclair

Harryboy Boas is a gambling man—the dogs. He lives in the quietly respectable streets of Hackney and keeps himself to himself. But then a new family moves into his building, with unsettling consequences. Step by step, the life he has led—with its own strange kind of order—begins to unravel. He is drawn into an underworld where violence and revenge stalk those who can't come up with the money.

"Lyrical, comic, truly original"
   TIMES LITERARY SUPPLEMENT

"A beautifully observed, understated study of an East End Jewish gambler… something of an underground cult"
   JOHN WILLIAMS, GUARDIAN

"Harryboy is a delicious and irrepressible companion…a tale as English as it is Jewish but with all the old Jewish virtues, humour, conscience and realism…It is what Harryboy would have wished—a winner"
   SUNDAY TIMES

"For all its hard and cunning realism this is an exceptionally moving book…a very fine piece of sensitive fiction as well as a tough slice of life… a very funny, racy book with a lot of insight"
   BOOKS AND BOOKMEN

Black Spring Press • paperback • 978-0-948238-45-1 • 192pp

King Dido
Alexander Baron

introduction by Ken Worpole

1911, East London. The police collaborate with racketeers to keep
an uneasy peace, periodically broken by vicious street wars. Dido
Peach comes to prominence running protection rackets by breaking
the unwritten rules of the underworld. His fall is just as spectacular,
shaking even the callous and vicious world he lived in.

"Enthralling"
   SUNDAY TIMES

*"Alexander Baron was a skilled traditionalist, a contriver of plotdriven,
socially perceptive meditations on place"*
   IAIN SINCLAIR

New London Editions • paperback • 978-1-905512-81-2 • 360pp

Rosie Hogarth

Alexander Baron

introduction by Andrew Whitehead

In the spring of 1949, Jack Agass belatedly returns from the war to
the working-class street in Islington where he grew up. A proud,
supportive community—with a pub and a barber shop, and a
common love of the Arsenal. But the street has changed. Jack
eventually finds his footing but he's haunted by a yearning for his
old childhood friend Rosie Hogarth, and for the pre-war security
and certainties she represents. Rosie has moved out and up—living
bohemian-style in Bloomsbury. He thinks she's selling sex—it turns
out her motive is political.

A taut and very human drama is played out through the summer
and autumn of the year. In his first London novel, Alexander Baron
provides one of the most powerful and compassionate evocations of
a working-class community in the throes of profound change.

New London Editions • paperback • 978-1-905512-98-0 • 352pp